THE MATIUSHIN CASE

THE
MATIUSHIN CASE

Oleg Pavlov

Translated by
Andrew Bromfield

LONDON · NEW YORK

First published in English translation in 2014 by
And Other Stories
London – New York

www.andotherstories.org

ISBN 9781908276360
eBook ISBN 9781908276377

A catalogue record for this book is available from the British Library.

Supported by the National Lottery through Arts Council England.

Published with the support of the Institute for Literary Translation (Russia)

AD VERBUM

CONTENTS

Part One   9

Part Two   53

Part Three   121

Part Four   207

Epilogue   245

Am I my brother's keeper?

THE BOOK OF GENESIS

PART ONE

It was as if all his life he had known in advance that what had already happened in it would happen again, so the memory of the past was more acutely felt – but the most memorable thing of all was childhood, although all that roaming round the garrisons after his father, the dreary rootlessness of father and son, the muteness and lovelessness, like an eternal lump in his throat, could simply have devastated him.

The children – there were two brothers in their family – had never known their granddads or grandmas, so lived without even the affection of old folks. The boys were born in towns far away from each other, in different times and, as if severed by their separate decades, they grew up as strangers.

This spirit of bleakness dwelt in his father. Grigorii Ilich Matiushin was born into the world already an orphan. For some reason, she who gave birth to him chose a graveyard to be delivered of her burden. And she probably wished death for her little child, wrapping it in a rag and abandoning it among the graves like a little corpse, only

11

because she was afraid to kill it with her own hands. But the bundle was found by people who had come to visit the small grave of their relatives. At the orphanage they registered foundlings with the names of those who found them. And so the anniversary of someone's death, which was marked by that visit to the graveyard, became his date of birth. That was all he could find out about himself as he grew up. He thought of those who had given him life as dead. However, with the passing years, they ceased even to be dead people for him. As a child he lived through the war, with its hunger and cold. Once launched into life, this son of the people, dreaming of qualifying as a mining engineer, worked in the same place where he grew up, in the Urals town of Kopeisk, in the coal mines, until he was drafted into the army.

The taciturn, austere young soldier found himself serving in Borisoglebsk, where he was accepted into the home of his company commander, a man of the same taciturn kind, who loved strict order. He was from peasant stock, a simple man, and he saw the young soldier as a son for himself, especially knowing that he had taken in an orphan. The commander had plenty of children, but all in vain, for he only fathered girls. His wife, who perpetually walked about with a large stomach, took no interest in keeping the home in order. The eldest daughter, Sashenka, managed the household and ordered her sisters about. She and Grigorii Ilich hit it off with no words spoken: he helped around the house, like a workman of sorts, and it turned out that he was always helping Sashenka: he was her workman and she fed him. She was sixteen years old and hadn't finished school yet. Grigorii Ilich had a year left to serve. The commander watched over his daughter carefully, and although he smiled, he used to tell the young soldier:

'You watch out, Grigorii, don't go staring, you haven't got a stitch to your back. That's not the kind of suitor Sashka needs, and anyway, she'll come in handy round the house yet. Let her help her mother, set her sisters on their feet, then she can get herself a bridegroom.'

However, things turned out the way that his dear eldest daughter wanted. One evening they were drinking tea at the family table, all present and accounted for, there in the commander's house, and Sashenka suddenly said:

'I'm going to marry Grigorii, I've got a child on the way from him. Do what you like, I'm going to have the child.'

The commander almost did for Grigorii Ilich, who went around black and blue for a long time. But there was nothing to be done. The time for Sashenka to give birth was getting close and, in another month, having served his full term, Grigorii Ilich could disappear from Borisoglebsk, and so the commander resigned himself to things. A boy was born and named after him, Yakov. He fixed his son-in-law up as best he could with a post in the bread depot. So Sashka stayed close at hand after all, still in the house.

But then suddenly she said to her father:

'Grigorii needs to study to be an officer, we're going to leave.'

Grigorii Ilich completed his studies and, from the time when he was given an independent posting, the Matiushins never visited Borisoglebsk, not even passing through, and they never invited their relatives to visit them.

They had to go to the funeral. But having shown respect for his deceased commander, Grigorii Ilich didn't want to let his wife go when the time came to bury her mother . . . Believing that he had achieved everything in life for himself, Grigorii Ilich was not so much proud of his own prosperity as afraid of letting his constantly moaning, bereaved relatives come anywhere near, even on a fleeting visit. Let them live their own life and we'll live ours. I'm not going to ask them for help, so let them not ask me for any. They've always lived at their father and mother's expense, so let them at least bury their mother, like decent people. I gave them money for their father, a hundred roubles to put up a gravestone – and all they do is make promises, the scoundrels, because they've eaten and drunk up all his money . . . He whinged on and on like that, refusing to let his wife go to the funeral, but he was surprised at how the anger, even fury, built up inside his Sashenka. She started shouting that she wasn't going to work like a dog, washing his clothes and feeding him, any more. Matiushin's first memory in life was his mother's howl ringing out in the dark, echoing house, when his father raised his hand to strike her but didn't dare to do it. At the time his father was cowed by the children, whom Matiushin's mother used as a shield to fence herself off – the elder son, an adolescent, and him, a small bundle at her unassailable feet of stone, his shoulders squeezed as painfully in her hands as in a vice.

This howl of his mother's tormented him afterwards, never settling anywhere in his mind. In their family the past was always subject to an unspoken ban, as if there had never been any other life apart from the one they were all living in the present.

Drinking alone after supper, Grigorii Ilich would sit on until late in the night, forbidding his wife to clear the dirty dishes from the table. Matiushin's mother would leave everything and go off to sleep, making the brothers go to bed too. The darkness took such a long time to grow, it was devastating. The silence tore down the walls and Matiushin felt afraid.

Nobody slept. On the other side of the wall, where their father stayed alone at the table, it was quiet. But they waited, not sleeping, knowing that the end had to come, the end that he was furiously approaching, torturing himself with vodka – and it would all end in weeping or a dark, hopeless fight between him and their mother. They never heard him come in. He crept into the room, as if he didn't want to wake anyone. But suddenly it would begin. Blinding, pitiless light. A wrecked room. Their father shouting his lungs out. Their mother yelping and screeching. Then something bursting out of the room, flinging the door shut. Silence would descend again, and the light would be obscured, then go out.

The boy recovered his wits in the arms of his mother, still breathing like an animal at bay and whimpering tearfully. But his older brother lay there blankly: he could endure the destruction and their mother's whinging, and his little brother wailing his heart out just two steps away. Their father couldn't endure it, but this son, their father's heartless shadow, could. And there were times when, after he got drunk, Grigorii Ilich merely sobbed forlornly all alone in the middle of the night in the kitchen, and his wife lulled him like a little child and led him away to sleep.

To Matiushin, his brother and his father were identical creatures. They even had the same smell: tobacco and eau de cologne. Yashka stole their father's cigarettes and eau de cologne, for which the father beat his elder son mercilessly, until he drew blood, punishing him for his thieving and again when he complained to his mother. And Yashka tormented his younger brother: he would grab his hand and squeeze it, crush it with all his strength, exulting because he knew that his brother would complain to their mother, and she would complain to their father. And their father would get him up in the middle of the night again, when he came back from duty, because there wasn't any other time. Leading him out into the kitchen, in order not to wake the others, he beat him as hard as he could, but Yashka gritted his teeth and endured his father's batterings. And that, it was fancied, made him grow up a bit.

Matiushin remembered his mother saying with relief that Yashka would soon be taken into the army ... Afterwards Yakov only wrote rarely from his posting. He served on the border, in some warm place somewhere: their mother retold his letters – and they immediately forgot about him. But Matiushin remembered how he dreamed that Yashka would be killed in the army in some war or other and never come back. Sometimes he fancied that his older brother really wasn't alive any longer – and because of that the walls of their home were papered with peace again, and a strict, neat order suddenly appeared in it ... Alexandra Yakovlevna boasted to her women friends: I tell Vasenka to sit on the stool so he won't get in the way, and he keeps on sitting there, the little sparrow, and I get all the jobs done and I forget about him. And he only felt good with her, the way it sometimes feels good not to think about anything and submit to everything thankfully, like a puppy.

With his service record, Matiushin's father earned rank after rank, post after post ... An abrupt, strong-willed, tenacious man who got everything done, he knew how to achieve his goal without stumbling and falling. Grigorii Ilich didn't fight to cling to his own perch: after a certain time he wanted only to win victories in life, and he could do it. This struggle required not only strength of will but the exertion of that entire will, which he achieved, transforming himself into a single, tense nerve in the form of a man. When father was sleeping, no one could make any noise, and at the table no one dared to speak; apart from him, no one had the right to leave even a spoonful, even a little bit uneaten. 'Who's this disdaining his bread? Who's got too finicky?' And what had been left uneaten was chewed up and swallowed as he watched – only then was Grigorii Ilich at peace.

Matiushin had eaten up since he was a child – choking as he did it, but eating up. There was fear in it, but a thrilling fear, contaminated with love, exactly like his jealousy of his older brother's closeness with their father – and the love, not the dread, made them subject to their father's will. This love could not be eradicated from their hearts. Just as their father failed to grasp that he was driving his children away and taking revenge on this alien life through his antipathy for them, so his children failed to grasp that the stronger it became – this antipathy of their father's, this sacred, bloody revenge that he was wreaking on life through sacrificing them – the more selfless and insuperable the impulse of their love for him would become, as if it were the very impulse to live, and they couldn't manage without each other.

When Yakov came back from the army, it seemed as if a new man had been born: courageous, resolute, bright and cheerful. Unexpectedly for everyone, his return to the family was a joyful occasion.

Grigorii Ilich's position could not have been more secure: a brand-new colonel, commander of a strategic division, he even looked solid and stately. At that time, during those bright days, Yakov's fate was decided. Grigorii Ilich had no respect for the labouring or even the creative professions, regarding one set as spongers and the other as blatherskites. And Yakov, like his father, despised weaklings – even at school, the only thing he enjoyed was the physical training: he lorded it over his bright and diligent classmates, who fearfully obeyed all his commands.

His years in the army had made Yakov physically stronger, and in addition the discipline had been strict, which had made him humbler, but clearly also because of that he had no interests in life, no desires, as if he were fettered somehow. The colonel was not averse to taking pride in his son now, but he was not so much thinking about Yakov as relishing the thought that the line of officers originated by him would be continued. The idea of Moscow immediately occurred to him – Yakov had served his tour of duty in the border forces, and the capital had the best border-forces training college in the country. In just one hour the colonel told his son how he saw his future life. Yakov seemed to be ready for this decision and gave his consent without a second thought, although it meant that he would leave the home, having barely had time to get used to it.

They left together but only the father came back, looking well rested and somehow without enough luggage. Yakov stayed in Moscow. He took the examinations – they gave him a place in the college hostel – and when he was enrolled, he could have left and come home to rest until autumn, but he chose not to: he set off immediately to the trainees' barracks.

To be on the safe side, Grigorii Ilich went to see the commanding officer of the college, so that they would know who he was. He spent the rest of the time looking round the capital, indulging himself in every possible way. He dined in restaurants. He stayed in the Rossiya hotel. He spent all of the large sum of money he had brought to Moscow with him. He came back, not in uniform, as he had left, but dressed completely in provocative new clothes, even with a beautiful yellow suitcase – he left the one he had taken with him for Yakov.

The moment the mother saw him at the door she went for him like a dog. Instead of joy, there was baying and howling. The child, who had been forgotten, first huddled in a corner, then darted out of the apartment. When it got dark outside and he started to feel afraid, he came back to a devastated home. Everything was smashed, slashed, ripped open. In the middle of the night his father showed up, totally drunk, out of his mind. He walked round the apartment, pleased with himself, thinking he had sent his wife packing. He prodded his son, but didn't wake him. Then he calmed down and plodded off to his room to sleep.

In the morning the mother came back, not alone but with support – a strange, unfamiliar woman who wept in pity for possessions that weren't hers. She helped with cleaning up the apartment, which was cluttered with displaced furniture and strewn with debris. When he woke up, the father left the women alone. He sat apart, tormented by his hangover and smoking in silence. The mother only shed tears over the Uzbek carpet, which had been bought recently: it was still as colourful as if it was brand new, but now it had a hideous slash right in the middle. Looking at her, the father started sobbing helplessly. He wanted to be pitied, but Alexandra Yakovlevna went back to her tidying with a fatalistic lethargy.

Calm settled in their home again. And from that time it seemed his mother and father's souls knitted together into one, as solid as rock. His mother bought another carpet and some new tall-stem glasses: she saved up what his father earned. Matiushin could sense this and he felt afraid of being alone, of being unnecessary to them. That was when he started missing his older brother and yearning for him. Grigorii Ilich had brought a colour photograph from Moscow, showing himself and Yasha, smart and spruce, standing in front of the Kremlin wall – the snapshot had been taken at the tomb of the unknown soldier. They put the photo in the best spot, in the china cabinet with the tall glasses and the father's gleaming army dagger – not for themselves, but for visitors, so that people would see it. Little Vasya used to steal the photograph for a while and secretly hide away with it in his room, dreaming of growing up soon and going off into a bright, new distance, like Yashka.

Yakov used to come visiting in summer, during his leave, but at that time Vasenka's parents sent him to summer camp, and they didn't visit him there – that was the order of things in their family. During those years his father gave up drinking and smoking and started taking care of his health, although he was still a long way from being old – which was why he was genuinely afraid of dying. Matiushin's father had put down roots in Yelsk: he commanded this little place that was almost an army town, and his authority there had long been undisputed. Ten years of living in the same place and with such great respect mellowed Grigorii Ilich. The peace of this little provincial corner, where he was the boss, inspired the idea of hiding away from life, surrounding himself with the little town that he controlled as protective cover.

The father's passion was hunting and then, after that, fishing – when he no longer wanted anything but peace – and he even came to love relaxing all on his own. But his two rifles, trophies from the Germans, remained in the home with him, even though he had got out of the habit of hunting. For as long as Matiushin could remember, the guns had been kept in the apartment, in their father's room, which no one dared to enter without his permission, let alone in his absence. There was a bureau in there that looked like a safe, made in times long past by a forgotten soldier craftsman. Every summer his father used to take out the guns and warm them in the sun, for some reason, and then they were cleaned and lubricated. Since he didn't like getting smeared with dirt himself, he trusted his son to clean the barrels with ram-rods. Matiushin performed this work with zeal, knowing that his father would call for him to bring the cleaned guns, then put them back in their covers and lock them in the walnut bureau with its only little key. The bureau, which he deliberately concealed from his son with his back, gave out the smells of leather, gun oil and something else. The bureau also contained numerous little shelves, drawers and boxes, and Matiushin only had time to glimpse their dark outlines before his father slammed the door shut and locked his property away, then turned round and drove his son out.

Matiushin fell in love with mystery, and he also fell in love with rummaging among things – his mother's buttons, for instance – and with hiding some things himself.

He grew up left to his own devices. Studying came easily to him, without any effort, but because of that he was tormented by boredom. The only thing that could rouse his interest in something was praise, but if he wasn't praised, he got bored again.

Very early on, Grigorii Ilich decided that he wanted his younger son to be a doctor, and not just a medic, but a specialist in military medicine. He needed a personal doctor, but someone close, and only a military man – as if a civilian couldn't have made sense of his health – and he wouldn't trust a stranger. If anyone in the family fell ill, they were treated in the infirmary: even the children were taken to an army doctor, otherwise Grigorii Ilich refused to believe in their illness.

In his early childhood, Matiushin had an earache and the army doctor, accustomed to simplicity, performed an irrigation and an inflation, probably damaging Matiushin's eardrum. At the time no one attached any importance to the fact that he became hard of hearing in one ear. However, many years later, at his first army medical exam, Matiushin was unexpectedly rejected because of his hearing. His loss of hearing was declared incurable, although he had grown accustomed to it in everyday life long ago, it didn't cause him any problems, and he was healthier and stronger for his age than his peers.

When he learned that his son had been declared unfit for military service, Grigorii Ilich didn't say anything for days, not even wishing to notice his son's presence in his house. He broke his silence with the words:

'He can't serve! Then what can he do, the little invalid? I thought there was going to be an army doctor in the house, but we've got a sponger instead . . . '

When his father gave up thinking about him and stopped believing in him, for some reason Matiushin felt better. He was prepared simply to work, without being afraid of getting dirty, and not come first in everything – which his father had been afraid of all his life.

For Matiushin, study and the path into the future were replaced by his job, but he chose the first trade that came to hand, a dirty and unattractive one – as a machine fitter. His father let him drop out of school without saying a word but despised him, jeering even when Matiushin gave his honestly earned wages to his mother.

'Look here, our breadwinner's home! To feed the lice.'

As for Yakov, their parents sent him thirty roubles a month and no reproaches were heard. Grigorii now recognised his own likeness only in his elder son – and in his heart he started growing attached to this thought, feeling an unexpected weakness for Yakov. In his final year Yakov didn't visit Yelsk. He informed his father in a letter that during his leave he was going to join a construction brigade in order to earn some money. They were sending him money every month from home and he had a stipend at the college as well, and how much did anyone really need in a barracks? And so Grigorii Ilich grew dejected. In autumn another letter arrived: Yakov informed his parents that he had married. He sent a photo of the wedding and a letter in which he explained drily that he hadn't wanted to involve his parents in the expense or to bother them, and that was why it had turned out this way.

In his heart, the father was glad that Yakov had reasoned like that. At that time Grigorii Ilich had developed a passion for saving money, amassing it in his Savings Bank book so that even Alexandra Yakovlevna didn't really know how much of it had piled up. Everything was turned into savings which he was too greedy to spend unless it was on himself: on his beloved Japanese spinners and fishing line, and once a Finnish sheepskin coat was bought, because he was afraid of taking sick in the winter in his ordinary coat. By that time the family was living off the state: Grigorii Ilich received a special food allowance as a member of the Municipal Party Committee and an army ration too. Alexandra Yakovlevna took care of the household. She already had to do everything at home herself or with her son's help – Grigorii Ilich strictly forbade her to use his soldiers, and if the question came up he would say:

'You've got that deaf one, rope him in.'

A rather stingy money order was sent off in response to the newly-weds' letter. No matter how closely they studied the photo that had been sent, the only person they could make out clearly was their son Yasha. They stood it in the china cabinet – yet another little icon that they could be proud of – and the young couple came to Yelsk and paid their respects to the father a year later.

'Everyone, this is my Liudmila!' Yakov thundered from the doorstep, and pushed his wife, who was displeased with something, into the parental home.

Liudmila seemed to be there entirely independently, on her own account. She was a tough woman, confident in her beauty, and her radiant body was curvaceously desirable, although she wasn't twenty yet: not even Alexandra Yakovlevna could bring herself to call her 'daughter'.

The power of love that she held over Yakov was obvious immediately. He was lovesick and never left her side, but acted as if he was in charge. In the home Liudmila respectfully kept away from Grigorii Ilich. She listened indifferently when Alexandra Yakovlevna gave them her matronly instructions about the best way for them to arrange their room and how to do the bed.

In Liudmila's presence Grigorii Ilich spoke only to his son, letting her know that Yakov was more important in their family, and pretending to look at the young woman in a quite ordinary way, although he felt uneasy as his glances scraped involuntarily over her breasts and thighs.

The summer field exercises were beginning, and the father was glad to take a break and set off for somewhere well away from home.

Everything had been arranged for the young couple – Yelsk was a deadly boring place, but every morning a little army jeep from the garrison drove up to the building and took them out of town to the river. Yakov and Liudmila started taking Vasenka with them for Alexandra Yakovlevna's sake. For the first few days she had set out, with a childish kind of joy, to relax with her family, as she thought of them. She had her fill of joy and then grew rather weary of it, but for some reason she wanted the young couple to keep going to the river with the younger son, if not with her.

Matiushin felt drawn to Yakov: he felt proud of having a brother like that but he also felt timid in the face of

Yakov's happiness. Yakov, who was a bit on the pudgy side, lounged on the river bank just as if he was at home and kept an eye on Liudmila, but all he wanted to do was sleep, and she wanted to swim and sunbathe. The languorous trips that the three of them made together illuminated Matiushin's life with such joy: new openness, the faith he was regaining in himself, in his life, in the immense world that had swung wide open. Without even realising it, this unfamiliar, grown-up woman suddenly became close and dear to him, undeniably unique. He could only turn his clammy, froggy skin inside out in his eagerness to submit to her. It seemed to him that now Liudmila was going to live with them for ever – and this summer suddenly rose up so bright and clear, so earthly and unearthly at the same time, as if it had sprung from under the ground.

Lounging on the bank, tired after swimming – and she liked to swim alone for a long time in the smooth water – Liudmila allowed him to knead and stroke her back and shoulders, which was pleasant for her and probably made her sleepy, although it set her young admirer trembling. But sometimes Yakov and Liudmila disappeared – Yakov took the little blanket and led his wife a long way away, to the tall field of maize, without saying anything to his brother, without even thinking of explaining anything. Sensing his little brother's perplexed glances, Yakov grew more irritated by his presence, and once his irritation erupted and he reproached his wife loudly when Vasenka was giving her a massage on the river bank after her swim.

'Don't you understand, you stupid fool, he's grop-
ing you!'

When they got home, Liudmila went dashing to pack
her things. Yakov mocked her and flung everything out
of the suitcase, and then, infuriated by her wilfulness,
he suddenly lashed her across the face, as if he thought
that would bring her to her senses. Little Liudmila stood
there and burst into tears. Hearing her crying, Alexandra
Yakovlevna ran into the room. Without a word, she flung
herself at Yakov before he could gather his wits and clawed
him as if she wanted to tear his throat out. Yakov froze to
the spot in fear . . . Coming to her senses and recovering
her strength, Liudmila put her arms round the mother
from behind and, acting fearlessly and pitilessly, dragged
the mother away from her husband as hard as she could.
Her strength, seemingly passionate yet also somehow
cold, free of any strife, immobilised the mother, who was
thrashing about in floods of tears. With the same cold
passion Liudmila nestled her lips against the back of the
mother's head, repeating that everything was all right
between Yakov and herself, and that she, Liudmila, was
to blame for everything. Alexandra Yakovlevna quietened
down. Small and dry, like a spider, she went back to the
kitchen, into her web, where she felt glad that the peace
of the home had not been destroyed. Liudmila took Yakov
off for a walk and they disappeared until night-time.

The next day Grigorii Ilich got back from the exercises.
No one in the house said anything. Oppressed by a feeling

that the place had suddenly grown cramped, he laughed, as if in jolly mood, and bundled the young couple off to the dacha to finish off their honeymoon there, well away from home. A week later, Yakov and Liudmila returned. By that time, tickets for the return journey had already been acquired, to let them know their hosts were tired of having guests.

There were a few days left until their departure for Moscow. They didn't go to the river any more. Out of basic indifference, Yakov ignored his brother's presence in the home – during those days he had many conversations with his father. Large and lusty, chortling toothily as they discussed the future, they sat through the evenings, and the father instructed the son as to how he should conduct himself and what he should seek to obtain from the army, generously and willingly recalling incidents from his own life, when he himself was just getting started in the service. He couldn't put a word in for his son; the border forces were under a different department, and Yakov would have to fight to be sent to the border he chose. Grigorii Ilich's advice was that he should start with remote and distant places, where it was easier to fight your way up, where the men got weary of serving; if that was a risk, it meant there was also a chance to show what you were made of. The Far East or the North. If he started with the West, in the Baltic or in Belorussia, where things were cushier, they'd gobble him up, walk all over him – the kind of men serving there were only safeguarding their own cushy spot.

On the day of the young couple's departure, no one saw them off – no one could violate the family custom. In their family people were only seen off as far as the doorway. But a long time was spent solemnly packing things for them to take with them.

All day long the mother piled up the hallway with boxes of jam, compote and pickles. With a soldier's help, they just about managed to load them into the car sent by the father to round everything off. The same soldier – the father's driver – had already been ordered to help them load up at the station, but Yakov suddenly announced that his brother would help them. It didn't make any sense to the mother that they all had to squeeze into one car and bump along, squashed up by boxes, if there was a soldier. Without even arguing with her, Yakov nodded to his brother, and Matiushin clambered into the dark bowels of the familiar car, feeling as if he was falling somewhere. They reached the little station at breakneck speed and unloaded everything onto the empty, deserted platform. The station in Yelsk consisted of two asphalt platforms steamrolled straight into the ground. Liudmila went off to one side and started waiting for the train on her own. Yakov searched the little station with his eyes, strode off and walked into some place without saying a word. Setting off after his brother, Matiushin found himself in a dimly lit station bar with a hollow echo. Yakov asked at the counter for cigarettes and vodka, taking a glass of it, so colourless that it seemed empty, and stopping at the first table he came to.

31

'How about you, don't smoke yet?' he said drearily.

'Yes, I do,' Matiushin confessed rather than answered.

'Let's have a smoke . . . Come on, it's all right with me . . . Maybe I can get you a beer, or you'd like something stronger, maybe vodka?'

'Yes!' Matiushin blurted out. 'Vodka.'

'Mind now, you decide for yourself, I'm not your father.'

Matiushin didn't say anything, and Yakov went for the vodka. He took a bit of salad on a little plate. And a bottle.

'If we don't finish it, there'll be some left, I'm not greedy. Right then, here's to the parting. Good health!'

Stunned by the ironic sneer he could sense in his older brother's words, by the fact that Yakov seemed to be saying: you and I are strangers to each other and you'll never be family to me, you little kid, Matiushin began pouring his heart out to his older brother in syrupy phrases, feeling as if he had divided up in the air of that bar and could see himself, like a reflection in a whole series of mirrors.

Yakov didn't say anything, just poured himself another glass. He cringed when his brother recalled their childhood, but Matiushin had to recall it, so that Yakov would know how Matiushin remembered him and himself to this day – as if he loved and cherished him. Yakov didn't want to understand that, or perhaps he couldn't: he didn't believe in that kind of retentive memory.

'You fool, don't you dare talk about all that, you're not old enough yet,' Yakov said intolerantly. 'It's all their fault! People like that shouldn't be allowed to have children, they maimed my life. And I can't make out who you think you are either. You say you remember me and you love me, but how can you love me, if I've hated you all my life? I started hating you as soon as you were born. I even remember the night when our mother and father fucked so they could have you. You don't know what I know, what I've seen . . . Our mother made our father the way he is. And what about the way he beat her? Stood her against the wall and beat her, because he didn't love her, because they've hated each other all their lives!'

'Yasha, they love you!' Matiushin whined drunkenly.

'They love themselves. Maybe they loved you too, you're a little mummy's boy, the way she raised you for herself.'

'I . . . I was never . . . It's you who's their pride and joy!'

Matiushin overcame his loathing for vodka and emptied his glass in gulps, right to the bottom, not knowing how to simply swallow it, flinging himself after his brother into the bleak, colourless abyss. At some unknown time he had convinced himself that his brother was unhappy, but maybe that was what he, Matiushin, had needed – not to see his brother as a strong being, but to see his pain and unhappiness through the strength and to pity him as he pitied himself. He even understood, *now* he suddenly understood, that he couldn't love his brother, but he forced himself to love him and to listen.

Without any kind of pain, only growing angrier and angrier, Yakov had his say . . .

'Our mother's just plain ugly, as if she wasn't a woman at all. She's like a grey mouse – not good enough for our father. All his life he's had women as easy as shit, any kind you like. But he never loved them. She knew that, so she wasn't concerned, she wasn't afraid, she let him stray. He beat her, he wanted to drive her to divorce him. He knocked her teeth out for that. But it was like they had a pact! When they had you, it wasn't children, it was ten-ton weights they needed to go on living with each other . . . And is that a life anyway, the way we lived, the way they live now? What have they got in their life? The kids? Why, I hate them, you, myself, everybody . . . The things I've seen! What can I think about them? What am I? A son, or maybe a son of a bitch, some kind of foundling? I know if I'm dying none of you will come: that's our custom – snuff it on your own. So I won't come to you either, you can all snuff it here! I'll live my life without them, without you: I don't need anyone. And that's the truth. There's no other truth, there isn't any truth.'

At that moment the earth staggered and a fine-splintered, jingling sound set the bar spinning. The glasses trembled and so did the huge-seeming, appallingly empty bottle. An inanimate rumbling was approaching out of nowhere, blow by blow. The air was already booming. Yakov grabbed his brother and dragged him out.

The Moscow train was trickling thickly into the little

station. The ponderous carriages rolled along the sharp line of the rails, windows flickered, a greenish, dusty ground floated by. The train stretched itself out and stopped. Yakov swore and drove his brother and Liudmila over to the boxes that had been left on the platform. They all grabbed boxes, suddenly becoming misshapenly similar, and ran – only Yakov got away from them, running forward, on and on, along the sheer wall of carriages. But there were no conductors to be seen at any of the blindly battened doors.

His brother shouted and hammered. It was as if they were all dying, as if they wouldn't let them in to breathe, to live! Suddenly a door opened in one carriage and the step was lowered with a clatter . . . A tipsy, condescending conductor looked down on them. Yakov tossed a box into the vestibule and jumped into its black opening, crowding the conductor. He yelled for them to hand up the rest of the stuff. Only his arms stuck out of the opening, as if they'd been cut off. Trying to keep up, not to fall behind, Matiushin jostled at the foot of the carriage, burned out from the vodka, breathing into Liudmila's snow-white linen back – she was grabbing the boxes out of his hands and handing them up to her husband. But the train shuddered and slowly set off on its way as if it was plodding along. Liudmila dashed in fright to a travelling bag that was still on the platform. The carriage was rolling away faster and faster. Yakov sprang out of the darkness, shouting, hung out from the step, grabbed the bag, then grabbed up his wife who was running after the carriage and hoisted her off the ground.

For a few moments Matiushin's eyes still clung to their carriage and he could see his brother, but Yakov vanished blankly into the opening, and the carriage disappeared in the smooth, even movement of others like it. He was still trying to run forward with the last box left in his hands, tramping loudly along the suddenly quiet platform, but he stumbled, went flying and collapsed three metres further on. When he came to himself, he could barely make out the train's little semi-circular, cast-iron icon in the distance. Reddish-brown compote was pouring out of the box underneath him. He guiltily unglued himself from the asphalt and dragged himself away, not knowing where to, thinking only of getting home as soon as possible. The dangling belly of his shirt had turned reddish brown from the compote's clammy wetness. Where the platform and the little world of the deserted station ended, all the paths and pointed-topped thickets of fences flickered in his eyes and the warm beehives of buildings glowed brightly – that was the suburbs of Yelsk, squat and broad, like the whole of the district. Two sober men who were striding along the street suddenly roared and started heroically chasing after him. Matiushin shied away from the men, alarming people walking towards him, and darted off into the courtyards and side streets, running until he got lost and then came to his senses in the middle of nowhere, in the twilight, on an empty lot overgrown with burdock.

He was carried home from the outskirts by a bus that laboured away until it was dark, wandering around for a long time, already half-empty, a bright spot in the hazy little town, as if it was meandering over the vault of heaven. Matiushin's soul was just as bright and as empty. He didn't sit, but stood in the corner by the doors, as if he'd been punished. People in the bus kept looking at him, some angrily, some pityingly, seeing a worthless, drunk young man with his clothes soaked in vomit.

The door was opened by his mother – in her night-shirt, with her hair dangling. She looked like a little kid like that, and her loose hair covered her head sparsely, as if it wasn't growing but lying on her.

'Have you lost your mind, gadding about until mid-night!' she asked, her voice soaring to a wail. 'Did you get there? Did you see them off? Did they get on the train?' With her weak sight she hadn't got a good look at him yet.

Not knowing what to answer, he hovered outside the door.

'What d'you think you're doing?' She dragged him into the house and then gave a shriek, immediately frantic. 'Son, son, what's wrong with you? Oh, Vasenka . . . What . . . What . . . Ah, you villain . . . been drinking, haven't you? You've been drinking! And your shirt, your trousers, what's that, what have you gone and done?'

Matiushin couldn't utter a single word, but he didn't want to stay silent any longer – he cringed as if he had been struck and started breathing hoarsely.

'Yashka, the villain, Yashka, it was him! He poured the drink, come on now, tell me!'

'Ya–a . . . sh-ka . . . ' Matiushin forced out, groaning feebly.

'Did he hit you? Answer me, what did he do to you?'

'Nn-o-o . . . No . . . '

'And the blood, where's the blood from?'

'It's from the box . . . It got broke . . . Compote . . . '

'Did they get on the train? And you? Have you been lying around drunk?'

But he didn't answer any more questions, he just gazed at her stupidly. His mother fell silent too, she'd run out of steam. Already thinking of something else, she shepherded him out.

'Go and wash, take everything off there. Quick now, or your father will come. It's just your luck, you villain, that your father's not in. Have a sleep, and then I'll give you a good talking-to, I'll give you what for, knock this nonsense out of you. You'll remember Yashka, oh you will.' And in her anger she lashed the shirt across his bare back. 'You'll remember him all your life!'

His father showed up: he clattered about in the hallway while he gave the mother instructions, then walked through into the kitchen, where she set the table. Matiushin was afraid to make a single sound as he lay there because his head was spinning as if he was being tortured on the wheel, and the bleary vodka haze was stifling him. But he endured this torture, managing to breathe and make himself fall asleep, he managed to do everything, even though he was poisoned with vodka. In the morning, when his mother interrogated him about Yashka, he lied to her, answering in fabrications, saying that he'd only asked Yashka for a sip in the bar, and kept mum about everything else. And so his mother cursed that train, and cursed his father for getting them tickets without places for a third-class sleeper, when he should have taken them to Gradov in the car and put them in a compartment carriage: there was another train that went to Moscow from there. And she kept mournfully recalling the particular box that had got broken – she'd only set aside one like that for them, with the jars of cherry compote.

Six months later the couple got in touch. They wrote to say that Liudmila was expecting a baby . . . Matiushin's father wasn't exactly delighted, but he trembled over that letter and made the mother read it out again, exulting that the line had been continued and joking that his little dacha had come in useful. Yakov was serving in a little town on the Polish border. He had set himself up, ignoring his father's advice, and he hadn't asked for any help. But as soon as the time drew close, the father seconded the mother to them with money, so that she could make sure they had all they needed for the baby and also stand guard over Liudmila and maintain order. The mother lived with the couple a long time. She stayed until the birth of a little girl, the granddaughter about whom Grigorii Ilich, strangely enough, had been dreaming. Knowing that this little Alyona was in this world, he loved her, not rationally, and not in an emotional sort of way, but with his blood. He went to see his granddaughter that very year, in person, after his wife. He considered this his duty also because Yakov hadn't obtained any accommodation in the little town and the young family was stuck in a dreary hostel. He used his visit to do everything for them: he got friendly with some people, bent over backwards where he needed to, gave some people a fright and some people presents – and managed to arrange a separate apartment for Yakov.

For a year, and then another, contact was maintained with postcards and letters, which Yakov wrote stingily, less and less often. But, having once made the effort to travel to such distant foreign parts, the father couldn't manage that kind of exertion again. His concern for himself, his desire for habitual comforts and – most importantly – for peace, were stronger. Looking out at him from the china cabinet, Alyonushka's photograph, with Grigorii Ilich in his dress uniform and medals, holding his granddaughter in his arms while Liudmila and Yakov stood at the sides like sentries, lulled him and put him off his guard. Many times he felt the impulse to go, but he didn't, and he wouldn't let the mother go either. They kept expecting Yakov and his family to visit them in the summer. Grigorii Ilich dreamed of how he would take leave and they would live at the dacha, how his granddaughter would eat raspberries and strawberries and he would take her fishing. The mother sometimes used to buy a toy, if she liked the look of it, or a beautiful child's blouse, or little woolly leggings or, if the price was good, a skirt or little shoes, storing them away to be grown into. But no one came. Then the postcards and letters suspiciously dried up. They thought: if there's no bad news, then at least they're alive and well.

Yashka showed up in Yelsk in April, 1982. On that day Matiushin was late, he'd had a couple of drinks, and he arrived in time to feel the air of invisible devastation in the home, the desolation, as if someone had just died. His father was in a bad way and his mother was fluttering around him, giving him something to drink to make him feel better. Grigorii Ilich was lying in an armchair with his head thrown back, looking up at the ceiling. And the first thing he said, in a pitiless, even boastful voice, was this:

'That's it. You don't have any brother. If he shows his face here, don't open the door, let me know immediately and I'll come – I'll fling that lousy dog out so hard, he'll forget the way back here and never show his face again!' The mother shed a few tears, and the father flew into a fury and shouted: 'Shut up, I've spoken! Who are you weeping for? Who's thrown away everything that was ever done for him in this life? A drunkard, a degenerate, a deserter, a bastard . . . Let him rot, the lousy dog, he'll never set foot in my house again!'

'But how can you, Grigorii. . . ' the mother sobbed quietly. 'Have pi-ity, forgi-i-ive him . . . Our little son . . . '

'It's over. He's finished. I'll give the order to the commandant's office, to the militia, let them catch him and put him in jail, the deserter. He's no son of mine.'

However, he couldn't bring such shame on himself. He waited, realising that Yakov might come back, preparing himself for the meeting. Matiushin also waited, in torment, although he couldn't understand what was happening. But Yakov didn't come. The father stayed at home and wouldn't let anyone leave, as if he were afraid. Yakov didn't come the next day either, or the day after that, when the father stayed to stand guard over the home again.

'Yashenka's run away from the army . . . His Liudka left him for someone else. She took Alyonushka away from us, took away my only granddaughter . . . Yashenka took to drinking . . . And your father drove Yashenka away . . . ' the mother wailed. But she kept silent when the father was there.

In a flash the two photographs on display in the china cabinet disappeared. Matiushin kept looking at his father, amazed at how calm he was. The only thing that mattered to the father now was to banish Yakov from his sight, to erase Yakov from his memory. And Matiushin had to forget everything too. On the third day, the father recovered. He felt even better than before, had a good sleep and ate his fill. He was so certain that Yashka was no longer in his life, or in Yelsk, that there was no more talk about him.

The doorbell rang, the mother went to answer it and there was Yakov. Maybe catching the smell of food from the kitchen, he lumbered in as if he owned the place and sat down at the table, dressed just as he was. Matiushin fell silent with his plate in front of him. His brother reeked of drink and the stubble on his face made it look dirty, even repulsive, as if Yakov had sprouted fur. He was wearing civilian clothes. But the hat, coat and shoes aged him and made him look pitiful. He didn't take the coat off, just sat there like that. His shirt collar stuck out like a dislocated wing. His tie dangled from his neck like a boa constrictor, orange and thick – a style that had been out of fashion for years.

'I see you're still stuffing your face . . . ' Yakov said tersely to his brother, and stared dismally into Matiushin's half-emptied plate.

Then the mother recovered her wits and said timidly:

'Why don't I give you some, Yashenka? Will you have some borshch?'

'Serve it up, mother! I love your borshch: no one in the world makes borshch like our borshch, the real article! Where's father, why isn't he at home?'

'Why, he hasn't come back yet.'

'Well, well, the old man's still serving, he just can't settle down. Give me the thick stuff now, good and thick. Don't be mean: there'll be enough for everyone. It's three days since I ate last!'

The mother didn't say anything, and he went into a

daze – and then he attacked the soup, gulping it down like a navvy digging, and after he'd dug a great hole in the plateful, he said:

'Come on, mother, serve me some more! Seconds!'

She answered him without moving from her seat.

'I haven't got any seconds, Yashenka. There's only enough left for your father. Go away, or he'll be here any minute now. Don't get him roused. You know your father: he doesn't want to see you.'

'What does that mean, he doesn't want to? Aren't I at home then? Am I sitting in some strangers' house, eating strangers' borshch?'

'You go back to your home, that's all. You've eaten for the journey, so go on. Afterwards, who knows: your father might forgive you and calm down.'

'So that's it then. You're telling me to fuck off, your own son?' he screeched, and started weeping shrilly, then suddenly hammering on the empty table, trying to crush it and smash it with his fist. 'Take that! Take that! Get out! Get out! Go and rot! Go and rot!'

Blood spurted. He held his hand up, stretching it out, showing it the way a child shows a little cut, and intoning in a meek, quiet voice:

'What have I done? Who have I killed, to be condemned like this, to have everything taken away from me? I love them, I love my father, I love them all! So why are they all killing me? She wanted to study, but I wouldn't let her, but this other one will let her, he's smarter, the child's not

his, he doesn't mind . . . He's got fine manners and I haven't.
He's got the right approach, he read her poems, the snake,
but I didn't! Why, ma, why? Why did you have me? Why
didn't you and father get divorced – then I'd have a different life, I'd be different, everything would be different!'

'Yashka, listen, don't you get started, do you hear me?
You've done enough shouting. Stop it, or I'll forget you're
my son,' the mother said harshly. 'Your wife left and now
look at you, sitting there bellowing, drunk. You've done
what you've done, you've got to understand that. And
there's no point bellowing, you can't undo it. You have to
live as things are, the way they've turned out. And why,
why do you want to go chasing after her – have you lost
your mind? You got your fingers burned once: do you
want to get burned up completely? Live, there's no one
stopping you. Just *live*. If you want to croak, then you will.
You know you don't need a father or mother to do that.
Get out of my sight, stop tormenting me.'

Yakov wept, quiet now, almost radiant. The mother
found a bandage and silently bound up his swollen hand.
He asked her pitifully:

'Ma. What should I do? They'll court-martial me, now.
I had no right to abandon my post . . . '

'Well, now, we're all equal before the law, and you
left your unit voluntarily, you have to understand that,'
the mother reasoned seriously. 'You go back, confess
everything, tell them it was like this and that, admit your
guilt, say it won't happen again. Only don't disgrace your

father: don't let the whole town know about it. And if you don't go away, he'll hand you in himself. But if it's voluntary, with a confession, they'll forgive you, and no one will even notice. You're not some private after all: you're an officer, they won't want to disgrace themselves. You haven't spent all your money on drink, have you? Have you enough left for a ticket? Well, look here, I'll give you some for the train, but if you spend it on drink, don't you come back, I won't open the door . . . '

The sight of this hunted man who was called his brother roused a scornful disbelief in Matiushin, as if he knew this man was only pretending and wasn't in pain at all. He couldn't forgive his brother for the words he had blurted out so thoughtlessly – and he sat there waiting for this unwelcome, drooling man to be gone from the table and the house.

Yakov vanished from their turbid period of hard times. Three years later, a zinc coffin arrived for burial in Yelsk from a foreign war too far away to be heard: that was how they found out that all that time Yakov had existed, lived and fought. Liudmila disappeared without trace: the family heard nothing more about her and Alyonushka after Yakov came to Yelsk and was cursed by his father. When they got the death notice, Grigorii Ilich was shocked to think that his son had turned out to be a hero. But the coffin arrived without any military decorations and the accompanying letter said he died in the course of performing his international duty.

The mother's grief was breaking her heart, but she couldn't sense the body of her son through the zinc: she didn't know, and so she couldn't believe that he was lying in that zinc container. It seemed as if at any moment Alexandra Yakovlevna would fall silent, stop crying, come to her senses and move away from the coffin. Matiushin understood that a terrible calamity had occurred, that his brother had been killed, but nothing stirred in his soul, and that made him fearful: his soul was living its own life, and it felt bleak and cold inside him. People kept doing things around him, as if Yakov had been dear to them. Matiushin stood there, feeling nothing but weariness – how hard and dreary it was for him to stand. His father kept a strict, stern face, standing near the coffin, but even now he couldn't bear to be closer than two steps to his son.

He was buried in the 'Soviet' cemetery, as the people called it, where they buried Party people and those who had served in the armed forces. The military commissariat was supposed to pay for the funeral, but the father wouldn't demean himself and refused.

From then on Grigorii Ilich cut himself off from his family. While previously they used at least to see him at the table, a new order was suddenly adopted in the house, under which the father ate alone. First the mother laid the table for him, then, when he went away, they finished up after him. And everything was like that. Matiushin had the feeling that he wasn't living but had sunk down underwater, where everything was murky and green, as if he

47

were seeing it through bottle glass. Now the despondency could stifle him for months at a time, making anything he did or any thoughts he had dreary and meaningless. And he lived without doing anything, not even knowing where the time went. From somewhere he remembered the ineffable light of life, its joy and the clarity, but when he tried to remember where the light came from, a bleary haze drifted up in front of his eyes, and what he knew wasn't that, but something different, and in that life of theirs, battened tightly shut, there wasn't even a chink through which to glimpse the light, and there was nowhere he could run away to from these four walls: he just lived inside them.

That spring, when Matiushin turned twenty-three, he suddenly received a notice summoning him to the military commissariat for a medical. When the two elderly medical-commission doctors rejected him again, all he understood was that he had been declared finally and completely useless. He walked out of the commissariat but he couldn't go home. His wanderings led him to the station, and there he found himself in the same buffet where he had once said goodbye to his brother. He recognised the buffet and ordered a bottle of vodka, as his brother had done then, drank as much as he could, then set off back to the commissariat.

In the doorway he started yelling that he wanted to serve in the army – but they wouldn't let him in, drunk as he was, so he rushed about, smashing and shattering everything in sight. Everyone on duty came running to grab him, even the commanding officer got involved. He calmed Matiushin down and led him into his office. The commander knew whose son he was, he knew his brother had been killed carrying out his international duty – but if only he could tell which decision would suit Grigorii Ilich and which wouldn't . . . He would probably have to guess.

'Is it really true a strapping hero like this can't be any use? We'll send him to the artillery: who needs keen hearing there?' he said, trying to sound cheerful. 'It's a family of heroes, a guardsman's dynasty, you might say, and we're blocking the lad's way. I'll settle it, I'll settle it . . . You stay at home and wait for the papers.'

Thinking that his father wouldn't find out, Matiushin decided to keep quiet about everything at home. He lived those days lightheaded with impatience, even haste, waiting for the call-up papers, but hiding from his father. One day Grigorii Ilich came home, weary and taciturn, and without even taking his coat off, just removing his shoes, called for Matiushin.

'I've heard that down at the commissariat you . . . You want to join the army? Get well away from here? Why, you fool.'

Matiushin's heart sank.

'Do you hear that, mother?' the father asked in a gentle, sing-song voice filled with indifference. 'It's happened at last, they're taking our boy into the army. They've declared him fit. His call-up papers have arrived!' And he pulled the notification out of the pocket of his greatcoat and slapped it down on the table: 'There, take it . . . '

Matiushin resigned from his odious job and in the week that remained to him, he did nothing. His mother didn't know what to do with herself. Alexandra Yakovlevna understood whose word had decided everything, but Grigorii Ilich never changed his decisions. And he responded to her weeping and screaming with a deathly silence – and remained silent until the next day. It was only then that he summoned his son to his room and recalled his own youthful days with him, and how he himself joined the army, then grew emotional and gave him the watch off his own wrist as a keepsake – the one that he hadn't parted with for ten years, the one he had bought for himself in Moscow, when he bought one for Yakov too, but that one had disappeared with his elder son. Only, left without the watch, Grigorii Ilich missed it, and in the morning Matiushin couldn't find it, but he didn't say anything: he felt sorry for his father.

In the morning Grigorii Ilich stayed at home to see his son off to the conscription centre. They didn't drive, but walked. The father was dressed in civilian clothes: grey and flabby in his raincoat, he didn't recognise himself and he felt timid. The recruits were being shipped out so early that they walked alone through the frozen, empty town into the gentle, twilit depths of the little streets. Alexandra Yakovlevna fussed over her own concerns, trying yet again to remember if she had put everything into the knapsack when she was packing for her son. She whispered:

'Listen, Vasenka, your father's going to give you twenty roubles from us. When you go to him, say goodbye nicely.'

Outside the military commissariat tipsy couples were jostling, music was roaring, everyone was saying goodbye. Grigorii Ilich strolled around off at one side, on his own, even striking up a conversation with one of the people seeing off a recruit, and waited. Alexandra Yakovlevna hugged her son, laid her head on his shoulder and wouldn't let go. They stood there like that until a non-commissioned officer as genial as a hostess invited the recruits to start getting into the bus. At that everyone clumped together in groups, people banked up like small snowdrifts, and all the mothers started crying . . . At the last moment Matiushin's father hugged him hastily, awkwardly allowed himself to be kissed, shamefaced, pushed the money into his son's hand and said:

'Serve well, son. Be worthy of your brother's memory!'

PART TWO

As night came on, the bus arrived somewhere. In the darkness not much could be seen except some tearful little lights: we'd stopped inside the fence of a distribution point. Inside, it was like a hostel, divided into little rooms: each of them contained beds with unstuffed mattresses and a table in the middle.

An officer walked in briskly with a red armband on his sleeve – there were lots of them striding about with those armbands, looking like volunteer public order militia. He ordered us to move from one room to another. Lots of young guys crowding the corridors; sitting along the walls, standing in queues at some of the doors, smoking non-stop, jabbering, and it's hard to believe it's night. They took us for the medical. And then, in the middle of the night, to be fed. We didn't touch the boiled grain but we guzzled all the watery tea, as if we'd been brought here to drink, not eat. We tried not to get lost any more, bunching up tight together. The waiting was wearing us out; we wanted to be on our way already – anything but carry on waiting. We weren't even let out for a breath of

air. Men jabbering on all sides, wherever you stand, striking up little conversations. The call suddenly rang out:
'Anyone from Kuznetsk! Over to the door!' – and everyone
fell silent and the crowd didn't move while every man in it
figured out thickheadedly whether he was from Kuznetsk
or not, and then whoever was got up in silence, escorted
by hundreds of already indifferent eyes.

An elderly officer with a jaded air appeared in the
room, a captain by rank, looking like a frog in his uniform.

'Is the Yelsk contingent here?' he asked, glancing
round as if he didn't know what he ought to do and was
trying to guess. 'Krivonosov, Konstantin Vladimirovich,
is he here?'

A disgruntled voice answered from somewhere:

'That's me . . . Here . . . '

The captain brightened up and glanced at his paper
again, hunting out the elusive, unfamiliar names like
little fleas.

'Is Matiushin, Vasilii Grigorievich, present?'

'Here . . . '

'Rebrov, Ivan Petrovich?'

'Here . . . '

The captain sighed in relief and said in a calm, almost
indifferent tone:

'Now, those men I named, follow me with your things.'

Matiushin straightened up and got to his feet, hearing the others get up too. They got up and walked out,
not believing that this was really serious, as if they had

no faith in the power of that dusty, froggy little uniform. Now they had to get up and follow it, walk after this little stranger wherever he told them to go. But they only marched about a dozen metres. Selected by some mysterious will, seemingly following some kind of schedule, they found themselves in another room, where there were about twenty other men with their things. The recruiting officer flickered erratically into and out of sight, disappearing and then surfacing out of the corridor with his catch – a new recruit – holding a roll call every now and then to settle his nerves. All the bureaucratic dithering made it hard to breathe, we were rapidly getting sick of all this waiting about. But the end of our time at the distribution centre was probably getting closer: to get us to trust him – no more and no less – the captain told us his name and patronymic and ordered us to prepare our things for inspection . . . He laughed when he found someone's t-shirt and underpants. He chuckled as he sniffed someone's eau de cologne. He was amazed by the food, all the different kinds of sausage, saying he'd never seen this kind or tried that kind . . .

They saw in the dawn at a railway station where they had been watched over in a half-empty waiting room for the rest of the night by the captain, now in a subdued mood. They were waiting for a train, but the recruiting officer stubbornly refused to say where he was escorting them, or even what branch of the forces they were going to serve in.

The little island of the blackly deserted station building was submerged in nocturnal darkness. Matiushin drank in the night, gazing out into the cold, anonymous expanse. Thrilled by the thought that no one in that expanse knew he existed, he even stopped breathing – it felt so sweet to be aware that there was only him.

Anxious, perhaps even afraid that they would run away from him, as morning arrived the captain ordered them all to line up. There was dozy jostling, another dreary roll call of names – by this time the word 'here' repeated in different voices was like a drill, boring through Matiushin's head. When the roll call was over, the captain led the ranks out onto the deserted platform. He ordered them to sit in a row along the wall, and started striding along the row like a sentry, waiting for the train.

It was already as bright as day on the platform, but they couldn't even hear the sound of birds twittering yet. Some smoked a bit, listening to this dead morning silence. Some dozed, slumped back against the wall, with their legs sprawled out across the asphalt, as if they'd been torn off.

Matiushin didn't remember their train arriving or how he ended up in the carriage. There was some kind of corporeal fire baked into his memory. He was woken by loud laughter in the hard-bunk carriage – for some reason everyone was calling it a 'berth'. And immediately he could feel that he was completely soaked in hot sweat. Jam-packed with men, the berth was like a furnace.

Streaming with sweat, semi-naked, his unsolicited friends were laughing loudly. And it turned out they were laughing at him: for sleeping like a log. They'd all got chummy with each other by this time, they were pals already, and they treated him the same way. It turned out that there was a bottle of vodka in the berth and they'd already drunk their share, but Matiushin's was still waiting for him. One young lad was bellowing loudly, acting more brashly than the others. Matiushin remembered him: he was from Yelsk, the recruiting officer had picked them out and led them off together at the distribution centre. Lanky and stooping, with a zero trim already, wild, ravenous eyes, dressed in absolute tatters.

Trying to fight the hazy weakness in his head as he heard about the vodka and realised he was on his way, in the train, Matiushin clambered down off the upper bunk. The berth fell silent. The Yelsk lad held out the bottle, thrusting it into Matiushin's hand. Warm from the heat, the vodka went down like boiled water. Or else he just imagined it was like water. All he wanted was to get blasted; he wasn't feeling anything any more. Instantly everything in his head blurred, the laughter thundered in his ears, and he started shouting something and laughing with the rest of them.

'My old man serves under yours . . . ' the Yelsk lad said out of the blue. 'My old man respects yours . . . So now we're going to serve together. You ask to be put in with me. Rebrov's my name!'

'You've got the wrong man. I don't have any father!' Matiushin chortled, and his new acquaintance went quiet; Matiushin couldn't hear him any more.

The drunkenness and the heat and the men all seemed like a single evil. They were being dragged off somewhere helplessly – this evil was being dragged off somewhere. Tormented by the evil, or so it seemed to him, Matiushin climbed back up onto his empty bunk and sank into oblivion, his forehead thrust against a partition that felt as cold as ice. He cooled off and fell asleep.

Rebrov shook him awake with devoted zeal, as if Matiushin himself had ordered him to do it. There was a dull glimmer of light. The sky outside the window receded in a uniform twilight blur. The train hurtled straight on, soundlessly, as if flying through the air. Rebrov had woken him to eat.

They were eating everything they had with them. They gobbled and drank without pausing for breath. The little table was piled high with sticks of sausage, pieces of chicken, cans, feeble May vegetables. There was wine and beer and vodka as well – and they weren't trying to hide, they weren't even hiding the bottles. This insanity must have started back in the afternoon, with that specially saved bottle of vodka, and then all the food and all the money had been thrown in. Hungry and only half-awake, grabbing at everything indiscriminately, Matiushin threw himself on the other men's food, swallowing lumps of something warm and fatty, and then flinging down his own 10-rouble notes on the common table when he remembered his father had given them to him for the journey . . . Rebrov topped up his glass and egged him on:

'Drink up – to Yelsk, our home town! And let them drink too – do you hear me, everyone drink to Yelsk!' he shouted to someone, and swung the bottle through the air, losing his drunken balance and collapsing onto several bodies.

The buzz of the inebriated carriage cheered Matiushin. After the food and the vodka he was feeling like a smoke, and Rebrov decided to lead him to the vestibule at the end of the carriage, clearing the way and acting pushy:

'Move aside! I'll clout you!'

Their squad occupied half the carriage, jumbled up together with civilians. There were lots of old men and women, all neatly dressed, strange, foreign, not Russian . . . They sat there, huddled in the corners, gazing with timid smiles at everything that was going on – at this gang of young, drunk Russian lads. Passing along the narrow corridor, Matiushin and Rebrov entered the dead end of the carriage, where the captain had taken up position, on duty at the door of the vestibule.

His hair neatly combed, almost slicked, he was sitting at an empty table without any food, reading a stale, well-thumbed newspaper on an empty stomach. His corner was full of the kind of secluded, strict order of which there wasn't even a trace in the open space of the blind-drunk carriage teeming with men. The captain probably had nothing to eat, he'd blown all his money. Free now after escaping from the restraint of his tunic, he looked more homely and younger; in his officer's summer shirt but locked into the captivity of the journey, he looked like someone on a business trip who definitely had nothing to do with the recruits.

'Comrade Captain, Fyodor Mikhailovich, we're off for a smoke! Permission to go out into the vestibule? Look, I've met a guy from my home town,' the Yelsk lad declared in sham delight, almost pressing up against the captain and reeking grossly of drink.

'Go and smoke . . . ' the captain muttered dourly and stuck his nose angrily into his newspaper, trying not to see their drunken faces.

The vestibule was packed with no end of people. They were roaring themselves hoarse, palling up, rejoicing at being taken off to serve in the forces – now that they'd realised they weren't going anywhere in the north or into the navy, but to somewhere warm – although the vestibule was as black and lonely as a deep pit. Matiushin listened, unable to see any faces through the tobacco smoke . . . Then suddenly he understood quite clearly that they were all afraid, afraid . . . That was why they were staggering about without any sleep, thrashing about in a sleepless, gluttonous fever, because they were afraid. Grabbing a bottle from someone, Matiushin took a gulp of vodka, but no matter how much he poured into himself after that, he couldn't get drunk – it all just seemed to evaporate. Even the reason he was feeling jolly wasn't the drink, it was because everyone around him wasn't sleeping but yelling, gorging themselves – going insane in their fear. Like seeing a crowd of naked people, and it's funny because they're naked, but still prancing about.

In the vestibule a non-Russian guy, one of those civilians, attached himself to Matiushin. He asked for a cigarette and started reminiscing about his time in the army . . . He was featureless and smooth, as if his face had been planed off. The only bright spot Matiushin saw was his mouth, which flared up crimson when the guy took a drag on the cigarette. Short, the height of a child, but stocky and barrel-chested.

'I've got two scars on my body from the army, and they knocked out my front teeth. But I don't bear the army any grudge. I think they did right to beat me. First, I'm an Uzbek, and lots of Uzbeks can be stupid; it takes a fist to make them understand anything, so they post them to a construction battalion. And second, if they hadn't beaten me, I wouldn't have done anything. If someone's beaten me, I respect them. I respect strong people.'

'An Uzbek! An Uzbek!' laughed Matiushin, delighted

that now he knew who was talking to him, and slapped the man on the shoulder. 'Come on then, tell me about it! I love Uzbeks!'

It didn't bother the man at all that Matiushin was giving him orders. That was what he wanted – to be needed, to hook on to someone. His speech was clear, pouring out from somewhere inside him. But his face, with its stony jaw muscles, was silent with a cool tension, not even human, and it guttered like candlewax in the glimmers and glints of transparent twilight from the blind end of the vestibule.

Matiushin started getting the kind of warm feeling he hadn't had with anyone for a long time. Drawing on this feeling of benevolence for the Uzbek, he felt a spiritual calm so strong that now even the stinking vestibule lulled him like a cradle. In this tenderhearted condition, he dragged the Uzbek after him back into the berth and tumbled out all his provisions for him. But the Uzbek kept talking on and on, telling only his own story and nodding dolefully, as if beating his head against an invisible wall.

For half the night they staggered from the vestibule into the carriage, from the carriage into the vestibule. And they weren't alone: no one was sleeping. Those who had drunk up all their money pestered those who could stand them a drink – and they didn't know what they were going to eat and drink tomorrow. Only the dirt-cheap cigarettes didn't run out. The hungry tobacco smoke swirled all around, as if the carriage itself was quietly smouldering, going up in smoke. The night stretched out, vastly longer than the day; it was impenetrable somehow. Its immensity made everything seem immense to Matiushin – the jagged, opened food cans, gaping like jaws; a gigantic human eye, flitting past as if under a magnifying glass; the vast space of the vestibule; huge two-legged people – and all the words that were uttered came hurtling out, flew through the air and fell like massive stone blocks.

He had long ago wearied of peering at the Uzbek and trying to make him out; he just heard his voice, sometimes distant, sometimes close . . . Some night or other, but a different one, not his night. A filthy, dark barracks; winter. A tunic has to be washed – a man has to be cleanly dressed. The Uzbek lays out the damp tunic, secretly washed after midnight, under his sheet and sleeps on it, drying it with his body, ironing it – he says that in winter using your body is the only way to dry things. Reveille. All around sleeping men jump up, tumbling off their beds like dried peas and dressing on the hop. The tunic's still damp, but it's smooth. The important thing is that it's clean and smooth – no one will see that it's damp. They're driven out into the frost to line up. The cold is terrible, ferocious. But for some reason the Uzbek is glad. Soon the tunic will freeze under his greatcoat, and then he'll stop feeling it and won't even notice that in the afternoon it's completely dry. That means the frost can act like the sun, can have the same power – so does that mean that heat and cold are the same thing? But the

the Uzbek carried on talking. Even if someone asks you to bring them a mug of water, refuse, don't do people any kindnesses. If someone falls, don't help him up, let him lie there, that way they'll bother you less. Think about how not to fall, not about how to interfere and be better than others. If you eat bread, think that you're eating shit, and if you eat shit, think that you're eating bread. Do the work you're told to do with a good will, be patient, but don't let them force you to do that work. Matiushin heard more and more fuzzily: don't have a lot of things, spend all your money as soon as you get your hands on it, give it all away, so no one can take anything from you by force or make you give it away. Respect the strong, acknowledge them, let yourself be beaten. If you don't respect them, they'll make you wish you were dead, or kill you. You have to live, think about nothing but living day and night.

Even though it seemed to Matiushin that in listening to the Uzbek, he had penetrated a secret that no one else in this carriage knew, all this still remained alien and unnecessary to him. He felt sorry for the Uzbek, but all he could do was say nothing, calm in the knowledge that everything would be different for him, the way he wanted it to be: it couldn't be any other way.

The vestibule and the berth emptied – lots of people were sleeping now. Those who weren't asleep kept on waiting and waiting for something, although there'd been no point in waiting for ages already, no one had any inner strength left. That night the train crossed a multitude of bridges, trundling over rivers. Almost every hour there was that heart-stopping, airy rumble, as if they weren't riding but flying high up into the sky.

The next twenty-four hours of the journey were over strange land – across the steppe. After the wild, drunken night, the bewildered men in the carriage gazed out of the windows, not recognising this land. Grey bushes and clay hills, clay hills and grey bushes. The captain said nothing about when they would arrive and where, as if he were keeping an important secret. They guessed in riddles:

'We'll get there when we need to . . . Wherever we're going, that's where we'll get to . . . '

Those who had saved some money started hanging on to it, and the implacable heat started driving everyone crazy. Men dropped on the spot without warning. The others poured water on them and they revived. Someone said they should drink more water, and the men dashed to drink not water but vodka, moonshine; they weren't interested in enjoying themselves, they just wanted to get blasted. That night fights broke out. In their drunkenness they smashed the windows in their carriage – to get some air. A bloody brawl started up, but the captain didn't interfere, he remained stoic and said nothing. Clumping together for a smoke in the vestibule, three or four men who were still on their feet and had lost sight of sleep marvelled at the captain's good nature. Why did he put up with it? Why didn't he take any notice? He only went once to the conductor who was selling the booze and he

They offloaded somewhere in the backstreets – in a corner formed by whitewashed fences with bulging coils of barbed wire along the top and bitty little buildings with no windows that looked like storehouses crowding in from the sides, as squat as if they had been hammered into the dried-up earth blow by blow. The small open space was scorching in the hot sun. They stood in a crowd beside the truck. Fresh, neat officers flitted in and out of sight, questioning the captain, who looked at them respectfully, no doubt waiting to be dismissed. Soon about ten sergeants were herded into the space from somewhere else and began standing guard, and the moment the officers went away, dirty little streams of soldiers started trickling through the sergeants' sparse line of security. Armour-clad faces, sunburned black, stared insolently, only it wasn't the Russians they were sizing up, but what they were wearing. There weren't enough officers to impose order. They'd hidden from the blazing sun in the patch of shade on the other side of the barracks, where little green trees stood like sentries and the parade ground, scorched to desert whiteness, began. There behind the barracks huts, a semi-naked, half-wild crowd had come running and gathered on the parade ground, and the officers allowed it to gape at the new arrivals and bawl and yell on the small, sweltering-hot islets of asphalt. From the parade ground the crowd could see what the officers had hidden away from on that side of the barracks: soldiers menacing the guards and working away furtively once they got in behind them, not wasting a moment to grab their booty, accosting the recruits who were better-dressed, intimidating them more and more brazenly by raising their fists and each snatching what he could.

And still the soldiers kept on demanding more and more, as if it was all theirs. One who ended up with a shirt tossed it onto the roof of a hut and went back to trying to scrounge or steal something else. Shirts, t-shirts, shoes, cigarettes, jeans, wristwatches – they took all these and then fought in screeching frenzy over who would get what.

Then the Russians showed up, looking for men from their own parts. They had white teeth and a sickly-sweet smell of eau de cologne. The officers let them through, probably because they knew them all by sight. The Russians had an aura of calm and self-confidence. Sitting down by the recruits, quizzing them crudely about where they were from, they struck up conversations and helped themselves to cigarettes, even if they couldn't find anyone from back home. They said they served in some kind of special platoon, the only Russian platoon in the regiment – there weren't any more Russians, only Ukrainians from previous drafts serving in the prison camp companies, and they'd been scattered around. That this was some kind of escort regiment. No one would have it easy in this regiment. And if anyone was put in the special platoon, he should soap up a piece of rope, that was what they said, grinning: we won't beat you on the first day, that's our custom, but afterwards go hang yourselves, you've had it, guys. They started driving home the very sensible idea that it was best to give any money to them now. After all, they were Russians, their own kind.

Matiushin's head was aching from its drunken spinning and he had a thirst more agonising than any he had ever known, so he kept thinking he could hear water gurgling. He was only distracted from it when a kind of scruffy beggar crept in under his shoulder, covered in filth from head to toe, so coal-black that even his round white eyes with red rims breathed out heat, like glowing coals.

'Kid, give us the trainers,' he said with a Ukrainian accent. 'Give 'em us, they won't be no good to you. I ain't got nothing and I walks over coal in the boiler room, come on, kid.'

'Just stop your whinging, will you . . . ' Matiushin managed to force out, and scraped off one trainer, tanned with thick dust that had turned it to clay. And then, with a sudden sense of relief, he freed himself of the other one and closed his eyes so as not to see anything any more.

A sensation of lightness entered his apathetic soul. He could hear everyone whispering about the bathhouse, but they wanted to drink, not wash themselves. And he fancied that there was a freezing-cold sea in the barracks hut, but when the hut was opened, they would choke on it. And only that morning hadn't there been a light breeze blowing over everything, but now it was midday and the sun was a blazing pillar in the sky and it had chained him to itself. That's it – the thought flared up and faded away again: everybody's thinking about the same thing, longing for the same thing – but then a tiny whisper trickled in from somewhere and there was a whiff of coal:

'Kid, kid . . . '

Matiushin opened his eyes. Like some little demon, the ragamuffin conjured himself out of the wall of the hut again right there in front of him. Smouldering joyfully, with his bony back curved over and his vertebrae glittering with coal, he pulled out from under his belly, as scarily as if it were his own liver, a dull mug or can, trembling with moisture.

'Tekit, have a drink of water. I've got lots, got a whole tapful in the boiler room. Cummon kid, tekit, it ain't infectious!'

Matiushin looked for a long time, as if he didn't believe it, but his throat contracted at the glitter of the bright, pure water, and he reached out a trembling hand for the can and took a swig from it, then took another swig – and he came alive, feeling the hard pebble of coldness clutched in his hand, giving him weight, transfixing him with a keen, smarting strength. Immediately arms were held out towards him like sticks from all sides.

'Give me a drink! Leave a bit of the water!'

He looked round – the scruffy beggar had disappeared in an instant, they'd frightened him off. Looking into the can – he fancied that it was still full to the brim – Matiushin forced himself to make that single movement, to put it into someone's hands. The small can passed noisily and joyfully from one man to the next and vanished.

'Water, water!' Matiushin heard, more and more faintly. 'Water! Water . . . '

Jangling her bunch of keys as if blessing the grey, stony yard with it, the mistress of the place arrived – a heavy-bellied, solidly built woman in a dirty white coat – and started yelling. She calmed down once she had driven off all the marauders; she enjoyed demonstrating her sternness to the new arrivals. The bunch of keys jangled as she brushed the flies away with it, shouting at them there in front of the unlocked barracks hut.

'You're for the bathhouse! I'll give you a proper steaming, you sons of whores!'

All the new arrivals were drawn up in a column and then ordered to walk into that hut. The cold crept across their skin little by little. The place had an empty echo to it. There were low benches running along the walls, a wooden perch. The woman, who had to be the supply manager or the stores manager, or perhaps just the bathhouse attendant, paused briefly in the doorway to get her breath back before descending on them and filling up all the space.

'Take everything off! Pull it off! Pull it all off, leave every part naked. No underpants now! You won't need them, you'll be issued with what you need.'

They got undressed and sat squashed together or stayed standing because there weren't enough benches. They jostled, scraping against each other. They didn't fold the clothes, simply dumping them straight onto the floor, and those who were standing, already naked, trampled them underfoot right there, beside the rucksacks and duffel bags. The woman watched with lively, sullen eyes, breathing heavily and shouting whenever she noticed someone hiding from her gaze.

'Bah, what a handsome buck! Why, I've seen so many men . . . ' And she ran her eyes over the floor, where the motley-coloured clothes were scattered.

She spotted something, stepped across, turned her backside towards them and bent down so that it swelled up in a huge downy pillow and the sumptuous curves of her flesh tumbled out from under her white coat. But when she soared back up as lightly as a piece of fluff and reassumed her shape, a quiet, cracked voice said:

'Tatyana, don't touch that.'

The man who called to her had halted in the doorway: he was short, thin and inconspicuous-looking, in a threadbare officer's shirt.

'Ah, come on, Sergei Lvovich, you're so quick to . . . Why, I didn't take anything . . . ' she whined like an old woman.

The officer moved to one side without speaking and stood by the wall. Soldiers appeared. In just their white undershirts, as if they weren't soldiers but kitchen hands, with fresh new boots dangling round their necks like bunches of bagels and lugging armfuls of foot wrappings and shorts, bundles of brand-new belts, heaps of rags. They carried it all in in a rush – and piled it where they were told by the officer, who called out plaintively from time to time:

'Konovalov, how are our linings?'

'Everything's top-notch . . . ' an implacable bass voice replied from out of the jostling crowd.

'Konovalov, so where are the stools?'

'Fuck it, Izmailov, I'll bury you; where are the stools?' the same boorish voice boomed out.

The soldiers rummaged silently in their own heaps, then immediately started on the abandoned civilian clothes, raking everything together from under the naked men's feet.

'Konovalov, come on, get started . . . '

A stool appeared from somewhere and a soldier with a forelock, who was stripped to his shorts, sat the first man on it. He stood behind him, seized his neck in his fingers, as if in a claw, and set to work with the clippers in his other hand, clenching and unclenching his fist. The man sat on the stool, naked as a corpse, and his hair showered down onto his body from the clippers. After the shearing he stood there, looking like someone else, doomed now, in full view of everyone – all the others had backed away from him in fright – and he asked if he should take his soap and bast scrubber. But Konovalov took him by the arm without saying a word, led him over to a little door, opened it so that it breathed out steam at them with a droning sound – and shoved him into the steam room, making everyone laugh.

The soldiers sorted through the kit without hurrying. The woman hovered close by, beside the things that were sneakily shoved to one side as still fit to be worn. The officer didn't notice that. The soldiers forced her back. They started yelling furiously:

'Where's that shirt you filched? You take it, you greedy bitch, and we'll take turns shafting you.'

'Ah, you little bastards!' She left the shirt alone and started complaining loudly and indignantly. 'Aren't you ashamed? I could be your mother! So I picked out a few rags; I didn't think you wanted them. Now just you try coming to me asking for soap!'

'Go choke on your soap, we've plenty of our own! What's not needed is lying over there; you keep your nose out of this pile.'

However, biding her chance in the tumult of the bathhouse, she kept picking things out of that pile and hiding them inside her white coat. Soon a large lump had formed in there. Waddling well away from the soldiers, she sat down furtively by the officer, sighed and laid her hands on her swollen belly, with her face lengthening as she calmed down.

'Grabbed a bundle?' the officer said wearily.

'What d'you mean? It's hardly anything: maybe I'll sew myself a housecoat out of the bits of rag . . . '

'I'll tell the supply and logistics commander to throw you out. I'm sick of this.'

'You punish me as I deserve, Sergei Lvovich! I've robbed the Soviet Army blind, but I haven't got a pair of drawers to my name. Look at the way you've shattered your own health, and they'll sack you without any pants too . . . '

The lobby of the bathhouse was emptying. The last heads were being shaved. Konovalov was working not so much zealously as lovingly. He loved his clippers, calling them his 'filthy slut' as he blew the hair off and brushed it away after dealing with yet another head. From the steam room came the sound of water and a babble of voices, abruptly interrupted now and then by patches of silence. Some men had already darted out of the steam room, wet from head to foot and as red as if they'd just been born into the world, and now they were queuing up to get their complete new kit from the soldiers.

Matiushin had been waiting his turn for a long time. Now he'd been overcome by the hungry, hungover shakes, and he trembled as if he was waiting to be sentenced. As he trembled with those hungry shakes he thought: what did I do to deserve this? Somebody needs me, don't they? I was born to live, wasn't I, just like them? Make my life dear to them too, make them take pity on me . . .

And then it seemed as if everything dissolved and he was sitting in the corner, naked, feeling like a stump of a man, with no arms or legs. The stool was empty. The soldier Konovalov turned round with the clippers in his hand.

'What are you doing squatting over there, like a bird on a perch?' But his exclamation didn't make Matiushin get up. 'Get over here, you weirdo . . . ' Konovalov said more simply now in his surprise.

Everything went quiet and everyone in the lobby turned serious. Only Konovalov dropped his hands helplessly.

'What's happening here? Just look at this walking wonder . . . Come and sit over here to get trimmed, I said.'

'No, I won't.'

'Why, he's drunk . . . ' said the officer, peering at him reluctantly. 'Look at the drunken face on him . . . '

But suddenly the officer started shaking with laughter. And then all the soldiers, and the woman, and Konovalov started laughing, their eyes goggling out so hard that the tears came; they couldn't stop themselves. And no one noticed that the officer had started gasping for breath, coughing, doubling over, hawking into his fist. Matiushin watched only the officer, mesmerised. It was all happening right there in front of his eyes: the officer broke down, no longer choking on laughter but on his own cough, huddling up into a shuddering bundle, and then he slumped off his stool, face down. The woman was the first to catch on and she rushed to help him up. They picked the officer up and sat him on his stool. He twitched silently as he grew calmer, restrained by the soldiers' hands. He was still short of air, his gaping mouth a black hole, his scarlet lips drooping, and he was struggling to say something.

His lips tensed and went limp as if they were straining, but the words had proved too heavy.

'That's it . . . ' he managed to squeeze out, struggling to recover his former serious bearing. 'That's it . . . K-ha, k-ha . . . What do you want? What are you waiting for? Konovalov . . . K-ha, k-ha . . . ' And he nodded. 'Do this one, get it over with . . . '

Matiushin still hadn't gathered his wits after what he'd seen. But then Konovalov, furious, rushed over and grabbed him by the hair. Matiushin crept along on all fours, naked, crawling away from the pain and seeing everything so clearly that his eyes smarted, even the chips knocked out of the black clay floor, hearing Konovalov's heavy panting above him. Konovalov dragged him across the lobby and Matiushin suddenly couldn't care less where he was being lugged off to or what they might want to do with him.

Afraid that he might escape, break free, Konovalov pressed Matiushin's head down against the stool as if he were washing it forcibly in a basin. His fist squeezed a metallic clanking out of the clippers and was gradually buried under a clump of hair. The bathhouse attendant surrendered to the languor that had spread through her soul and gazed at Konovalov, admiring the way he froze, motionless, leaning down over his work, and the way his whole body curved, seeming to reveal a hidden inner strength, becoming covered all over with knotty muscles. Matiushin wheezed regularly, gulping at the air, staying down on his knees with his cheek crushed against the stool, running his blank, unseeing gaze over the crowd of half-dressed, half-naked men who were either admiring or frightened by him.

'Oi, I'll die laughing! Oi, that's the way they strip the bristles off a wild boar! Don't you go and strip the skin off him, Petenka . . . ' the woman exclaimed merrily, and her face turned radiant and serene with merriment and excitement.

'A strapping great boar!' Konovalov grunted in reply, as if complaining.

When he heard that, Matiushin felt happy, almost proud of himself, and forgot about everything, no longer aware that he was down on his knees with the clanking clippers tugging out his hair.

Konovalov finished his work but didn't let Matiushin go: his blow tossed Matiushin over to the feet of the soldiers, who had been waiting just for this and threw themselves on him. Blunt kicks from boots showered down on Matiushin's naked body. He came to his senses and called to them, imploring:

'Guys, don't hit me on the ears . . . Guys . . . '

'Stop that! Konovalov!' The order rang out suddenly and the blows subsided.

The soldiers who had been beating him moved away and Konovalov, who was afraid of nothing, but obeyed the officer who had spoken, helped Matiushin to get up and led him to the steam room, intoning under his breath:

'Have a good soak, buddy. Feel the thrill, you bastard ... '

Scalded by his beating from the soldiers, Matiushin skidded into the steam room as if he was slithering down an icy slide.

Men who had already settled into the warm womb of the bathhouse were walking about with small tubs, moving from one tap to the next and splashing water on themselves. When the water toppled out in a solid block from the tub raised over Matiushin's head, he huddled up tight – and breathed out so deeply, it was almost a groan, and then thrilled to the pleasure and stroked himself with his hands. All around there were untaken tubs, gaping open. Colourless, hot and cold streams flowing. The roaring of these countless torrents set his soul trembling at the gills, like the soul of a fish. Matiushin dissolved in that roaring, nuzzling his mouth at the icy cold water disintegrating into spray, spurting out of the tap so hard that his lips went numb. He drank his fill, gulping down water straight out of a tub that was full to the brim, snuggling up to the calm, smooth little lake, barely able to hold the weight of it in his hands. Feeling as if he hadn't just quenched his thirst but found peace and freedom, Matiushin held his tub in his hands and wandered round the hut, which was rippling, mirage-like, with little pools and streams. He found a small piece of coarse rag and a small abandoned piece of soap. He washed. He sluiced himself off from the tub, tempering himself with the cold until he was blue. He got tired.

After the steam room, the air in the lobby was so light
and easy, it took his breath away. The lobby was filled with
vigorous, swarming merriment. The men laughed at each
other, stroking their own unfamiliar naked craniums. They
clambered joyfully into the loose official-issue trousers
and tunics that were now theirs, feeling a new freedom
in them. Everything was issued too large, for the wrong
size, apart from the boots; they only stuck to the right
size for the boots. The soldiers from the quartermaster's
section laughed when they saw what the parade looked
like. In the crush, Matiushin was given everything in
the very biggest size, and on top of that they issued him
with a knapsack. He squeezed through the scrum, found
a place on a bench and got dressed, following standard
procedure. Only he hadn't been taught how to wind on
the foot wrappings – and he sat there crumpling up the
two rags in his hands, with no idea of what to do with
them, with all his buttons already done up, but barefoot.
But others who were as ignorant as he was spoke up. The
officers shouted for the sergeants, who had been loitering
in the yard for too long, and it turned out they were keen
to teach the men. Some sat down on the bench with lads
they liked the look of, others stood over a small bunch of
barefoot men and gave them orders on what to do from
above. Matiushin was spotted too: a sergeant squatted
down a bit and emerged from the bathhouse bustle in a
tunic that was scorched white, with a faded little red flag
tucked into his belt. He smiled, looking at Matiushin, and

just arrived from some place called Karakemir, from a
boot camp far off in the mountains, way off on the other
side of the world, where they'd been pounded into shape
as sergeants. They tried to look tough, putting on a brave
face, but it was clear they were having a hard time in the
regiment. The officers asked confidentially if they had any
complaints and did anyone want to go to the jakes. Then
suddenly a little officer came running up and announced
that he was the regiment's Communist Youth League
organiser, collected the League members' cards, still panting, and ran off again.

They walked through the Tashkent regiment's desert
base in a now fresh, green, brand-new army column, trying
to look like soldiers. Acting as its guards, the sergeants
strode along at the sides with little flags, and two officers
strode briskly at the head of the column, chatting chum-
mily. At the checkpoint, a grubby, tattered, downcast-look-
ing sentry opened the gates for the column, then shouted
and pulled threatening faces as they left. The humpbacked
roofs of the barracks and the camp's fences fell further and
further behind. The column crushed the silence beneath
the clatter of its boots. They strode along a shady street
that seemed to have no beginning and no end. Kids they
guessed were homeless ran about freely here, playing in
the roadside dust. Women who looked like Gypsies gazed
out from warm, blossoming yards with little low fences
in which the gates were flung wide-open. White-bearded
old men emerged from their homes, while behind them

the lavish gardens, like bright trimmings round their calm, ramshackle mud houses, exploded brightly into the hot air, resting their light, fragrant branches on the old men's shoulders. Soon the old town disappeared in the haze and the blueness of the steppe, with its greyish tint of grass and plants, opened up to its full extent – and they strode across that steppeland, scattered, each man on his own, towards some point on the horizon, towards which a line of immense, wide-branching metal pylons retreated, pulling their high-voltage black threads across the sky.

Flasks were supposed to be issued to them at Dorbaz, so they walked without water and as evening came on they crept into the camp dirty right up to their necks and panting with thirst. Dorbaz was three long, spindly, freshly painted plywood barracks huts. A patchy puddle of rolled asphalt, withered in the dry steppe, was the camp parade ground in front of the barracks huts. The place was empty and dead, but it turned out that the camp was having supper. The new arrivals lined up on the parade ground, and the sergeants came out after supper to join their buddies who had been away for a day. Here in the camp they were more important than the officers, who immediately disappeared. The senior sergeant, whom everyone called 'the Moldavian', even to his face, walked about in flip-flops, undershorts and an army hat, as if he was on the beach. He held a knapsack check.

The sergeants stood and looked on good-naturedly to see what various bits and pieces had arrived in Dorbaz with the knapsacks, but they didn't attempt to take anything. They would filch it all that night, which was why they were so genial now. The senior sergeant just confiscated a can-opener from someone and strolled along the line-up, toying with it, tossing it from one hand to the other and explaining his laws – and he was affable, because he was explaining those laws for the first and last time. Matiushin didn't hear a thing. His feet were on fire with a pain so bad, it felt as if they'd been shoved into a furnace. Standing was even more unbearable than walking. Matiushin thought he had to endure this pain – that was what he believed every other day too, as he re-bound his blister-tortured feet in their blood-soaked wrappings during a moment's break when they were allowed off the parade ground, and then the Moldavian's favourite command would ring out smartly:

'Co-o-o-mp-a-a-any, fall in! A-a-at the dou-ou-ouble!'

When they had been out marching around the parade ground for hours and the weaker soldiers – who weren't even soldiers yet but half-soldiers who still hadn't sworn the oath – were dropping with sunstroke, unable to take the forty-degree Asiatic furnace, they were got up on their feet and back into line with the help of sal ammoniac supplied to the sergeants by the army doctor. Drinking water was trucked in. A cauldron of water was boiled up with desert acacia collected out on the steppe, and everyone was given a flask of this sticky, nauseating tea to drink every day. It wasn't possible to drink much of it: only a swallow, and besides that, the boiling water had only cooled off a bit and no one felt like drinking something hot. A tank of water for technical use was moored behind one hut, by the kitchen. This water was taken from wells in the steppe and it was tainted with infection, dangerous to drink but, either because they wanted to get infected and end up in hospital or because they didn't understand, at night many of the men would sneak over to the tank and drink from it.

In addition to the Russian draft, there were Armenian, Georgian and Ukrainian drafts in training, or 'quarantine' here: about a hundred men. During the day the officers walked to the village (its name was also Dorbaz) and filled themselves so full of tea in the *chaikhana* that when they got back to the camp in the evening, they just flopped onto their beds and slept like dead men. For them the month of quarantine was penal servitude in exile from their families, from a better life. At night the sergeants went to the village. They bought hashish and moonshine from the locals and had a high time in the barracks until dawn. After getting stoned, some spent half the night trying to extort money for a hangover cure, while others spent half the night torturing and passing judgement on those guilty of offences under their law, allowing those to whom they took a liking to smoke hash and drink moonshine with them for the rest of the night. To amuse themselves they held battles in the passageway that ran in a broad strip between the beds. Young Russian, Georgian, Kazakh and Armenian guys – some intimidated and some plain terrorised – fought tooth and nail while the bombed sergeants giggled.

The most brutal atrocity was the safety tax imposed on the half-soldiers by the Moldavian. They all had to line up and then the Moldavian would punch every one of them on the left side – on the heart.

The sergeants told them that this blow had long ago made the Moldavian famous in the regiment. After his punch your heart might stop, and only another blow from him could make it start working again. Even if that didn't happen, the Moldavian's brand would be there on your chest – and he was very proud of it, that bluish mark left by his fist. He was also fond of saying that that was what the heart was like – the size of a fist. But one night something happened that everyone saw, and Matiushin saw it too.

The Moldavian reached the middle of the line, where the Georgians were standing, when suddenly, after taking a punch, a man dropped dead. There was a horrified hush. Already stepping on to the next man, the Moldavian flung himself at the crumpled body, roaring and bellowing, no longer a man or even an animal, and started working away so furiously with his fist that in an instant he'd turned crimson and was running with sweat. Who can tell how many men prayed at that moment that the Georgian wouldn't come back to life and that would put an end to the Moldavian's amusement? But suddenly the little Georgian jerked and started breathing ferociously, his eyes already wide open, and the Moldavian ordered the frightened sergeants to pour him a glass of moonshine and walked on, drunk on what he'd just experienced, to pound all the others anywhere he fancied, working off his fear. Matiushin would suffer ten of those blows, over ten nights . . . They made everything go dark in front of his eyes.

Although they called the training centre a concentration camp and a disciplinary battalion, there was a certain bravado in this talk, as if, without even noticing it, they somehow managed to feel proud of themselves and this deathtrap of a place. This was why they squabbled blindly with each other over all that was best there and, if a Russian offended a Georgian or vice versa, a bloody battle would immediately erupt right there in the barracks or on the parade ground, and crowds of men fought frenziedly. Matiushin never had time to understand what made these fights flare up, and many of the others also didn't understand, although they still went rushing off in a crowd to crush the foreigners. But Matiushin always felt his life was coming to an end in the daily torment on the parade ground. His foot wrappings and tarpaulin boots were the same as everyone else's, but once he'd made the first march from Tashkent to Dorbaz, his feet had been transformed into open wounds. Everything had started wrong for him, and Matiushin didn't understand what it was that he'd done and the others hadn't; why were their feet all right? But they had announced at the very beginning that anyone who got bloody feet wouldn't be treated, but punished. The Moldavian had another rule like that: if you wanted to go to the infirmary, then you would pay the price at night before you went back to the regimental barracks. Matiushin endured his suffering. The commander of the infirmary was a tooth doctor from the regiment, sent to Dorbaz for the summer months, and he worked indefatigably – day in and day out he bundled off to the regiment men with jaundice and those who couldn't be got back on their feet and into formation even with sal ammoniac. But Matiushin's endurance, or his health, were stronger than the jaundice, stronger than the broiling sun. His suffering deprived him of the desire to eat and he just chewed on his bread ration, three chunks of bread a day.

One day they were herded off to drill as usual, across the steppe and round the camp. Hard as he was trying, Matiushin fell behind. The sergeants turned the platoon, which had run on a long way ahead, and drove them all back to Matiushin – and as soon as he dropped behind by a hundred metres or so, the whole thing was repeated. The soldiers dragged themselves along, the formation groaned and wheezed, but no one dared glance at Matiushin, although he could sense their explosive internal resentment as his gaze crashed painfully into their dirty, mute faces running with sweat and their blank backs swollen up

dashed over to him, lifted him up and led him away to
the camp. He couldn't speak, but only howl in pain. It was
clear that Matiushin had injured him badly, but even so
they couldn't start exacting retribution from Matiushin
in front of the entire formation, in front of a crowd of
witnesses, and anyway they still didn't know what form
their retribution would take. They just ordered him to
fall in. The command to run rang out again, as if they
had decided to finish the drill. But the sergeants bringing
up the rear drove the platoon on with their boots, so the
men at the back crowded onto the ones in front, driving
them on in turn, in order not to be beaten. Matiushin
realised what they were doing to him – the entire platoon,
guys just like him, drove him along, desperately forcing
their fists into his back, no longer parting around him.
The sergeants didn't tire. At the most terrible moment,
when he felt as if he was going to break down and fall,
Matiushin suddenly felt someone at his side, preventing
him from falling, helping as much as they could, holding him up. It was Rebrov, silently gritting his teeth and
lugging Matiushin along, and someone else he didn't
remember or didn't know, a little red-haired soldier who
was using his body as well as he could to hold back the
pressure from the men who were pushing forward as
they were beaten by the sergeants. Matiushin held on,
but when Rebrov and the redhead had no strength left to
drag him along, he broke down and ended up plodding
along in the rear of the platoon, where the sergeants in

'So what's all this? Got too much strength, don't know what to do with it?' the commanding officer said, looking up at him from the bed. 'Do you know what they do here to people who don't know what to do with their strength? I'm talking to you, comrade soldier: answer!'

'No, sir . . . ' Matiushin declared through his stupor.

'Moldavian, why is he so slow-witted? You're a really bad bastard. I entrusted the company to you; do you go about with your eyes closed?'

'We'll handle it, comrade Captain. I have my procedures.'

'Handle it, handle it . . . I know about all that business. You've turned the barracks into a den of vice. Just remember: if need be, I'll have your hide, and you can go to hell, I don't give a damn about you.'

'I won't go to hell,' the Moldavian retorted. 'And my hide's tough enough to handle it.'

'Get up! And get out! And don't you go getting cocky, or I'll cocky you! You'll cocky yourself into prison camp, have you got that? And explain to this fine fellow of yours where all roads lead to!'

When they emerged from the stuffy half-light of the officers' tent, the Moldavian didn't hurry – he smoothed down his uniform and drew himself erect. He ordered Matiushin to walk forward, to the latrine. The hump of the little adobe shed stood on the outskirts of the camp, a long way behind the barracks, as grey and dried-up as the steppe. Matiushin remembered only the loud buzzing of the flies: there were as many of them as bees in a hive. The Moldavian pressed him hard up against the wall with his chest, but didn't hit him; he only spoke in a powerful whisper:

'I'll call for you tonight, and then you come, without any fuss. Better on the quiet. There are plenty like you in the regiment. They have a good life. They get to guzzle their fill. If I take a shine to you, I won't let the others have you, you'll be mine.' He stepped away and stood menacingly over the toilet to relieve himself.

The sergeants probably knew what kind of justice there would be that night, what sentence the Moldavian had pronounced. They stared at Matiushin cunningly and every last one of them kept shouting: 'Better hang yourself! Better hang yourself!' But Matiushin couldn't understand what they wanted to do to him.

The thought that they could kill him wasn't frightening: if the Moldavian killed him, then later the Moldavian would be killed for that. In fact *he*, Matiushin, was the one who had been born to kill *him*.

He was already delirious; a mysterious fire was devouring him. The camp was wearily living out the remains of the day in hungry anticipation of the evening roll call, remembering the rations that had been eaten at supper and not the long night that was approaching. Rebrov appeared out of nowhere and sat down on the bench beside Matiushin. He smoked a whole cigarette he'd got hold of from somewhere through the teeth at one side of his mouth, like an old hand. He didn't talk about anything, he just kept quiet, as if he was a stranger, which was true in a way, because ever since the train, Matiushin had shrunk away from him. And before today's events the two Yelsk men had avoided each other here in the camp too.

'So that's it, then. We could have gone to NCO school together. I told you: stick by me, but now it's goodbye and farewell,' Rebrov hissed, looking round. 'There's still time. Clear out of the camp . . . '

Matiushin remembered being woken by a searing pain. In a cold little room flooded with light where the air conditioner was rattling its box, in the infirmary. He was pressed down onto the couch, facing the ceiling, and the army doctor was straining to pull a boot off his swollen foot.

'Alive? Grin and bear it then, if you've come round!' the doctor said in a very loud voice. 'No, we'll have to slit the boot . . . What have we got for cutting?'

'There's a knife,' someone's voice replied in a humdrum tone.

'Bring it over . . . Slit it there on the side, and don't tug it or he'll bawl.'

'But what's wrong with him?' another voice, curious, drifted down from the ceiling.

'It's you who should be asked what's wrong with him! He's got raw steak for feet. Haven't you got anything better to do, you savages?'

'Has anyone even touched him? No one's laid a finger on him . . . He probably slashed up his own feet and pissed on them – the bastard's trying to wangle his way into hospital, to fill his belly.'

'Who taught him to piss on his wounds? You, sergeant? You should have taught him how to wind on his footcloths!'

'He knows that himself, he's as smart as they come.'

Something plumped onto the floor like a rat. The pain subsided and through his drowsy state Matiushin heard the voices talking.

'That's it for me . . . Take him into the sick bay . . . '

'But all the beds are taken in there. Where can we put him?'

'You can leave him on the stretcher; he'll stay there until morning. Only don't leave him in the passage, you fool, find a spot off at the side.'

He felt his own weight – they lifted it up and carried it, panting.

'Oo-ooph, the bastard . . . He's getting off on it . . . Right, up you get! Get up!'

'Shut it, you . . . The senior lieutenant will hear you.'

'But he's just getting off on it, getting off on us carrying him . . . '

'When we get him there, we'll drop him; only flesh and bone isn't he, let him snivel . . . '

They dropped the stretcher in the dark and laughed raucously, because Matiushin did what they intended and roared. Beds round about started creaking and bodies in them stirred and came to life.

'They've woken up! Want to eat, think I'm going to feed them!' the male nurse laughed. 'Don't know if it's day or night, those jaundice cases!'

'Come on, rise and shine, you bastards!' the sergeant called merrily. 'A flash over there on the right! Gas, fuck it! Lie down! Get up!'

Cheerful and delighted with himself for giving them a fright, he sauntered off, listening to the scraping of his own boots, and issued a command into the deathly darkness.

'Okie-dokie, stand down. As for you, footless wonder, don't sleep, we're coming visiting tonight. Oh, we'll be visiting you all right . . . ' Matiushin heard in his black hole.

Everything went quiet, but in his agony Matiushin didn't believe that the sergeant and the male nurse had gone. So he waited. The darkness breathed, lying doggo, until a glassy transparency appeared in it – and then, no longer trying to find those other two, Matiushin began weeping at his own helplessness, at being dumped alone on the bare floor, far away from the little white clouds of the beds. But his tears weren't heard and there was no one to rescue him. He fancied that the bare blackness was not the floorboards but the night itself. The little clouds were melting, melting . . . He crawled off the stretcher and, dragging his useless legs along, without even knowing what he was doing, crept in under one of the beds, as if he was squeezing into a crack, and fell quiet there. At night they came, he heard the tramp of their feet, their drunken, bovine wheezing, their whispers. They were probably too drunk to make any sense of what had happened to him or where he'd vanished to, and they couldn't get away with making a racket by rummaging about to find him.

In the morning the ambulance from the medical unit came to pick up its cargo. That was when he was missed. They searched right through the camp for him. It was obvious that no one in his condition could get far, even if he crawled. The tooth doctor pumped the male nurse and discovered that the new soldier had had visitors in the night, and then he beat out of him who those visitors were. The ambulance stayed where it was parked. The Moldavian and three other sergeants were summoned to the tent, where the officers, who had just woken up after a drinking session and were in a vicious mood, beat them mercilessly until they lost consciousness to make them tell the truth about what they'd done to the soldier during the night – after all, they could have killed and buried him. The Moldavian toughed it out, although the officers pushed him really hard, aiming to break him and not even concerned that he might croak. The other sergeants faltered, broke down and let out a few things about the Moldavian and what he did to the men. And so in the fever of that morning they started interrogating everybody, holding the Moldavian secure in the tent – and, not seeing him around any longer, the folk came clean.

The jaundice patients found a man, half-alive, asleep under a bed, but when Matiushin was discovered, the top brass no longer had any time for him – he was dragged out, dumped on a stretcher and loaded up.

They loaded up another stretcher too, with the injured sergeant – and they lay side by side. The ambulance hurtled across the steppe and they suffered torments in the jolting, bouncing vehicle. Matiushin groaned. And the sergeant, for whom groaning or moving his jaw was impossible, whined dully, clutching at the stretcher. The sweat streamed off him. He was exhausted by the pain, he was suffocating. They reached the regiment at breakneck speed. Matiushin was offloaded into the infirmary, and his bog-green, slashed boots that looked like toads were flung onto the stretcher – and those toads sat on his chest, watching over him all the way to reception. They offloaded the sergeant, who was in rather worse shape, and wheeled him further on, to the hospital.

Matiushin moved from the stretcher to a couch on his own and was able to get undressed when they told him to get all that filth off him: he used a towel moistened under the tap to scrub down this unfamiliar body overgrown with moss – himself – the way a male nurse told him to do. He heard the concerned army doctor talking about him:

'Why is it we have this wasteful management at every turn? Tell me, Verochka. They take a man into the army,

but they don't teach him how to wind on his footcloths . . .
It doesn't look like he did the job deliberately, does it?
What do you make of it, Verochka?'

However, they didn't give him anything to put on.
They told him to lie on a trolley and pushed him along
head-first in front of them, which set everything spinning
and swimming about.

On the operating table Matiushin fell asleep without
any anaesthetic. He slept for twenty-four hours or even
longer and, during that time, they dripped donated blood
into him from a bottle and nourished him with injections
of sweet water. He slept sweetly, dissolving like a lump
of sugar, with the orphaned blood flowing through his
veins. But after he had slept right through the day, he
seemed to sense that the night had come and the anticipation of a call slipped into his mind and was driven home
firmly. Drowsily preparing to jump to his feet, he woke
up, unaware that he was lying in an infirmary instead of
a barracks.

Everyone in the infirmary had to work, attending to
their own needs and those of the army doctors. Matiushin
was issued a pair of crutches and ordered to get up. His legs
were bandaged up to the knees, as if they'd put a pair of
white felt boots on him. He found it hard to stand on the
crutches. The first thing they told him to do was provide
a sample of urine. The male nurse gave him a little may-
onnaise jar with no lid. Matiushin stuck it in the pocket
of his dressing grown and tottered off to the privy. He

made a real effort to manage the jar, but he just couldn't do it. All he could do was pull down his underpants, but when it came to setting the jar in place, his hands couldn't cope, the crutches kept slipping out from under his arms. He put the jar on the windowsill and hobbled over to the metal urinal – after all this hassle, he couldn't hold out any longer. A downtrodden-looking guy with his head shaved in crude steps, as if in deliberate mockery, ran into the privy to relieve himself. Holding the jar in his hand like a stone, Matiushin barked out hoarsely:

'Listen, brother, you're not infectious, help me out with these samples . . . '

The downtrodden guy docilely did everything required – and disappeared. That was a load off Matiushin's mind. Now he had to carry this stranger's urine to the male nurse, but it spilled in his pocket while he was hopping and dragging himself along, and the male nurse wasn't slow to speak up when he saw the wet patch on Matiushin's side.

'What's up, bro, not pissed yourself, have you?'

The folks in the infirmary lined up in the little garden; the infirmary sergeant-major, a haughty soldier with a moustache who wasn't sick with anything – in fact he was the plumpest, best-fed, healthiest of them all – gave the orders, striding up and down in front of the line. Some called him the 'boss' and some the 'foreman', like on a building site. He handed out work to everyone and, not bothering at all that Matiushin was on crutches, he told him to sweep the paths in the garden. Matiushin refused to do it, right there in the line-up. He thought the foreman was making fun of him. The foreman walked up and lashed him across first one cheek and then the other, with his open hand; Matiushin couldn't even raise his hands, he couldn't lift them off the crutches even to protect himself. And the foreman carried on lashing him across the cheeks until the lad next to Matiushin intervened – he shielded Matiushin with his body and persuaded the foreman to let him take on the job instead.

Next day the foreman ordered Matiushin to sweep the paths again – this time Matiushin kept his mouth shut.

The day after that Matiushin saw what happened when someone was discharged from the infirmary. They discharged a Kazakh – he'd been there for a long time, working as a dishwasher. He was striking to look at and belligerent, the kind that people here said was 'on the make', like in the prison camps. He'd fed himself up around the kitchen cauldrons all right and got free and easy, but when the foreman hissed that the army surgeon had ordered him to pack up his bits and pieces and leg it back to his company, he dissolved into a pitiful, shapeless lump in front of everyone's eyes. At lunch they could still see his puffy, crimson face in the serving window, but the foreman didn't like that – the fact that he hadn't left yet. The foreman finished his lunch calmly and let the others finish theirs, then he went into the snug, dark little room where the cook and the dishwasher worked – and everyone heard a loud racket and horrendous screams. They all stayed there, waiting to see who'd get the best of it, no one interfered. About ten minutes later the commotion in the catering block stopped. The foreman appeared, dragging the battered kitchen worker along the floor by his hair.

'I told you, didn't I tell you, to clear out of here before lunch? You were asked nicely, right? Decided you were smarter, did you?' the foreman harangued him, feeding his fury with his own words.

'YabastardIllkillya-a-a!' the dishwasher screeched.

'You . . . Don't you go making out you're mental!'

Everyone standing about doing nothing came alive, wanting to get it over with quickly, to smack down this old buddy who no longer mattered to anyone.

The words showered out of every mouth: 'What were you told? Didn't get it, did you? You didn't get it, you scumbag!'

A week later, they suddenly took Matiushin's bandages off altogether. His feet had healed up. Only he couldn't understand what good they were to him like that – healthy – now that they'd taken away his crutches. Now that he was well, not doubled up over crutches, Matiushin felt useless and doomed. All that week he'd worked – sweeping the paths in the garden, standing duty on the ground floor where the menials lived, running errands for the doctors, lugging medicines and papers about whenever he was sent for. But when they took the bandages off and the crutches away, he retreated to his own floor and hunkered down there, not knowing what would happen to him. The foreman sauntered around that floor without noticing him, and Matiushin was in torment, wondering if there was an order for him to be discharged and what the army surgeon would say. But that evening the foreman called him over and gave him a job to do.

'First thing tomorrow you scoot over to the catering block . . . I promised the cook I'd let him have someone, but watch yourself, you try swinging the lead – and I'll have you over in the latrines in a flash!'

Early the next morning, the cook met Matiushin with a knife in his hand and wouldn't let him inside the door of the catering block, making him stand outside among the empty tables. This skinny little Uzbek, who looked like a fourteen-year-old, seemed like a harmless little snake, creeping about but unable to bite. Finally he condescended to let Matiushin in, told him to sit down, thrust into his hands a bowl containing pieces of cold pork – actually from the cabbage soup at lunch – and sliced up half a loaf of bread. That was how he showed that he was good-natured and could even be generous with chow if he wanted. Matiushin wasn't hungry, but he started chewing away willy-nilly – tucking in and taking a look around. The little Uzbek was pleased, thought he'd tamed him. He came up to Matiushin's chest and they were only the same height when Matiushin was sitting down.

Inside, the catering block was just that, a block – square-shaped and faced from floor to ceiling with glassy tiles. It was like a sauna in there: the room got no air, only the hot sunlight. The heat was nothing to the Uzbek. Deciding that his assistant had gorged himself enough, he showed how fierce he could be by grabbing the bowl out of his hands without any warning and barking, baring his teeth, to make him stand over by the sink.

It wasn't even a sink but a huge vat with aluminium kitchenware dumped in it. The little Uzbek jumped up and sat on the high windowsill, looking down on Matiushin as he worked. When the pans and huge cauldrons had all been washed, he ordered Matiushin to wash the floor and watched him again as he crawled around with the rag. When the floors had been washed, he showed how good-natured he could be again and gave back the bowl of food: Matiushin was already hungry, or perhaps it was rage sucking at his insides. Then the little Uzbek pulled on his cook's outfit over his skinny little snake's body and shepherded Matiushin out with him – it was time to take the trolley and push it over to the regimental mess for the rations.

Walking outside the infirmary fence felt as strange to him as being in the streets of an unfamiliar town. On all sides, no matter which way his eyes turned, there were barracks standing blankly on guard, asphalted paths stretching out to make mysterious connections, identical little trees growing. They didn't meet anyone until they were approaching the mess, when they ran into a crowd of soldiers. The little Uzbek drew himself up and stuck out his chest and started shouting, to goad him on. The cast-iron trolley turned stiffly on its three wheels. Matiushin was dragging it from the front, so that he looked more like a dumb animal than anything else. The food cans clattered against each other with a dull chiming sound, and the crowd stared at them in a way that made Matiushin uneasy. The cook ran up and thumped him hard on the back with his fist. The soldier lads hooted approvingly. They started shouting: 'Go hang yourself! Go hang yourself!'

In the immense chef's kitchen, which could have swallowed up a dozen of their catering blocks, there were three boiling cauldrons that looked like wells and everyone who was hanging around near the mess gathered to take a look at the quarantine soldier. Every last one of them looked like Matiushin's little Uzbek, so Matiushin lost sight of him. Matiushin dragged over the large food cans with noodles, and soup from one of the wells was poured into them by their downtrodden lackey, perched up on a stool in soldier's fatigues so dirty that they were brown. The lackey bustled like a little cockroach, delighted to be right there with Matiushin in full sight of everyone. He gave Matiushin orders in their language, and the Uzbek cooks standing around laughed. No one said a single word to Matiushin in Russian, and the fun of it all was that he didn't understand what they were shouting at him, in fact he did just the opposite of what they wanted. When they were getting the bread, the breadcutter, a big, strapping Uzbek with a bull neck, asked what his name was, and when he heard it was Vasilii, he was delighted: his name was Vahid, which was kind of the same. He was so pleased, he said, that he was making him, Vahid-Vasilii, his little brother, and from now on he would help Matiushin in the regiment, and Matiushin could call him brother: he demonstrated with a rumbling laugh how a brother and his little brother should embrace each other when they met.

The little Uzbek withdrew into his shell when his assistant and the regimental breadcutter became brothers right there in front of him. The two of them took the loaded trolley back to the infirmary without a word. The noodles were kept ready on the stove until supper and, after supper, Matiushin set to work again. The little Uzbek was in a nasty mood, he smoked and didn't do anything, but Matiushin worked like he'd never worked in his life before. It had already got dark outside, the infirmary was sinking into sleep, but Matiushin had to take a container of the day's waste to the mess on that same trolley. The little Uzbek, staggering about with his big knife in the silent, empty catering block, smiled with a drunken smile that had appeared out of nowhere . . .

Following the route that he scarcely remembered and could barely make out in the dark, Matiushin trundled the trolley to the mess, where there were soldiers on fatigue tinkering drowsily with something. These soldiers, who had probably been herded here on the sly to do some kind of dirty work, swarmed round him from all sides; they wanted to make him do the work for them. They kicked and mauled him until some powerful man appeared out of the night: a single glance from him sent them creeping off into various corners, back to their jobs.

Matiushin dragged himself back to the infirmary, drove the trolley into its stall, trudged off to his own floor and into his ward, where he fell into a deep, work-worn sleep. And early in the morning, when everyone was still sleeping, the little Uzbek, who looked as if he hadn't slept a wink and could hardly even speak, woke him up – it was time to go off to the regimental mess for the rations.

Three times a day he fraternised with Vahid, drove the trolley to the regimental mess and washed the tableware, the kitchenware and the cauldrons. At midnight, when he took the waste to the mess, the hungry, cowed soldiers from the kitchen fatigue were waiting for him. And from early in the morning he languished in the catering block, deprived of something more than mere freedom, left one-on-one with the little Uzbek.

The Uzbek wasn't very bright and everyone yelled at him because he was so slow on the uptake. But all the yelling had no effect at all: he remained deaf. His job in the infirmary was a doddle because he didn't boil or roast anything, except maybe for his friends and himself; he got the rations ready-cooked from the regimental mess – the only thing he did was cut the bread with the huge knife that he never let out of his sight.

The cook spent all day sitting in the catering block, going out at night. It turned out that he was a local man – home for him was a collective farm outside Tashkent, and his wife and younger brothers came to see him every other day, bringing food from home. They also brought him cannabis, which he hid in a little pouch under the stove. He'd probably gone crazy ages ago, visibly withering away from smoking this stuff. The cook smiled stupidly and said nothing, but that was the madman inside him, cunningly hiding, keeping shtum and smiling. If he got any kind of feeling, for instance, if he was suddenly afraid, then the fear overcame him completely, filling up his soul so that it flowed over – and he could be frightened to death just like that by an empty saucepan clattering on the floor. He couldn't actually work; he couldn't even be forced to work. He didn't sleep at night, because he couldn't sleep unless he smoked himself into unconsciousness. And there was a special significance to the fact that he never ever put down his knife: the huge bread knife was the only thread that bound him to life, without it he couldn't feel or understand anything. He was killing himself, but it was as if he was playing with death, which had become impersonal to him, it was everybody's – but nobody knew that. He lay in ambush for Matiushin when they were alone together in the catering block, waiting for moments when he bent down or sat on a stool, and then skipping up to Matiushin from behind and setting the large blade to his throat. The first time this happened, Matiushin night, until Matiushin felt like he was answering the little Uzbek through his own delirium. The cook, half-dead, as if someone had been torturing *him* all night there in the catering block, eventually sank into oblivion, finally letting go of the big knife. He sprawled on the floor, like a sleeping dog. Matiushin kicked him in resentment, but then lugged him off to his bed – everyone in the infirmary was still asleep – clearing him away like a corpse.

After sleeping all day long, the little Uzbek dragged himself to the catering block when it was already almost evening and everyone had finished supper ages ago, and reached in under the stove, where he hid his grass. Matiushin, standing at the sink with his back to him, caught the odour of hash fumes snaking and coiling round the catering block. Then the cook started wandering about, still not saying anything, wandering on his own, with the big knife . . . He crept stealthily about behind Matiushin; sometimes Matiushin could hear his footsteps and sometimes they disappeared . . . Matiushin hit him on the hand, knocking the knife out of it, then grabbed hold of him and dragged him along, scattering kitchenware with a clatter – and he beat the little Uzbek, believing he was killing him, revelling in every sound that burst out of that puny, rotten little body.

'I'll kill you! I'll kill you!' Matiushin howled, almost passing out at the piercing, agonising sweetness of it, dragging the half-dead cook about and flinging him against the wall. 'I'll kill you!'

And those words brought Matiushin round: he recovered his senses.

The cook was hardy and he began to stir as soon as Matiushin left off. Soon he even perched on a stool.

'Now you just sit there! Sit! Got it?' Matiushin shouted obtusely, as if at a dog. 'Just who are you? Who are you? You're a dumb desert bonehead, that's who . . . Come on, get up! Get u-u-up!'

The stunned little Uzbek forced himself to get up and started crying soundlessly.

The cook could easily have got someone to get rid of the Russian, taken his revenge on him so that there wouldn't be a trace of him left in the infirmary, but he swallowed everything. And it was all repeated day after day – the two of them bleakly incarcerated in the catering block, the cook's oblivious stupor, and these drubbings. However Matiushin now beat him with deliberate precision, knowing the moment when he should thump him hard and he would quieten down. The cook really did quieten down, but he almost always cried, as if some kind of poison seeped out of him with the tears. These outbursts of weeping made him repulsive to Matiushin, who treated him like his own assistant, except that Matiushin did all the work himself, for the two of them, disdaining to coerce the little Uzbek.

Matiushin took the bread knife away from the cook, hid it in a place of his own and didn't let the cook get hold of it again. But the little Uzbek put up with this apathetically as well. What Matiushin couldn't take away from him – he was afraid to – was the grass. Out of a kind of spite, he started smoking it himself. The cook gave him dope on demand. The little Uzbek wasn't actually burning up grass that he had paid for; it was free. Soldiers who looked like wild beasts used to come to see him on the sly. When they arrived, they sent Matiushin away and talked about something in secret with the cook and sometimes even beat him. The cook didn't say what they beat him for. He looked just as dejected and desolate when he was called for a meeting with his wife and brothers and someone else – who it was, he didn't say.

Matiushin spotted a tattoo on the shoulder of one man in the regiment: it was a snake, coiled round a sword that was lying on a shield that looked like a chevron, and this shield was framed by an inscription: 'I serve the law'. He managed to find a handyman in the infirmary who drew the tattoo for him, and only took two cans of stewed meat for the picture. Now the chevron with the snake decorated his shoulder too. Although what law it was that he was willing to serve he didn't understand. He liked the snake, the shield, the sword . . . When the foreman saw the tattoo on his shoulder, not healed up yet, a mass of scratches, he lashed Matiushin across the face with the back of his hand once, and then again, in front of everyone in the mess.

'Have you forgotten who you are? What law is it that allows you to go flaunting yourself around here, you

lowlife? That's it, I'm throwing you back into the regiment.
You'll be licking out the privies with your tongue . . . They'll
teach you, if you haven't learned already . . . '

Matiushin avoided anyone from Dorbaz who ended
up in the infirmary. The downtrodden young guys, about
ten of them, who were blown in like dirt, amounted
to nothing in the infirmary – anyone could push them
around or hassle them and, more than that, everyone
tried to make one of them into his own personal lackey.
Sometimes he fed them in the catering block, but only
because the food turned his own stomach. Behind his
back they repaid him for this with their united hostility,
although in his sight they sucked up to him, thinking
that otherwise he wouldn't give them anything. Secretly
they thought the way he stuck with the cook was a dirty
trick – they all thought that he was the same as they were
and had betrayed them.

But one morning for some unknown reason a great
commotion broke out around the infirmary . . . A whole
crowd of officers – staff officers – came running, and everybody else was running around too, an incredible hullabaloo
erupted. A whole platoon had come from Dorbaz. His own
lads, Russians, the ones he had started with in the army,
in the same platoon in quarantine. Their tunics had faded
to white from the sweat and the salt, and their voices had
a low drone to them, like the hot fire in a stove.

'So this is where you got to!'

'Look here, it's Vasilii! Vaska! Vasyata!'

'Boy, oh boy! Hi, how're you doing, brother, you took off on the quiet!'

Matiushin looked around, blind-eyed, but they laughed and surrounded him, patting him from all sides, healthy and genial; it was as if they'd suddenly sprung up out of the ground.

'Well, why don't you say something? We remembered you, we remembered you every day! We'd have had to put up with that bastard, if not for you! The Moldavian was sent off to a disciplinary battalion! You didn't know that? That's where he belongs, the scumbag!'

'Yes, brother, you'll never go back to Dorbaz again . . . And we're moving on to be sergeants, but we'll descend on all of you in the autumn, with our badges, to give you some backup. Just hang on in there until then.'

'If you see any of our guys, say hello, we'll be back to give them a hard time! Ok, live like a man!'

An officer showed up and summoned the soldiers, who had clumped together into a tight group, and they promptly obeyed.

Suddenly the infirmary felt empty. The dry, hot air meandered aimlessly inside its walls, and Matiushin didn't feel like a man any more – or like anyone at all. He went back to the catering block, his heart calm and empty. When he'd done his work, he went off to get the lunch, pushing the trolley, not recognising anything in the base, forgetting this regiment more with every minute that passed and somehow surprised at his own decaying memory.

The mess seemed to him like some kind of barracks, an anthill of soldiers. When he reached the bread-slicing room, he looked at Vahid without saying a word, almost as if the powerful Uzbek was a pig, as if he wasn't standing up level with him, screening off the bread room, but sprawled out amongst the bread, grunting. But Vahid greeted his little brother with simple-hearted joy, took his time issuing the bread ration for the infirmary and, without noticing a thing, embraced Matiushin until the next time.

Matiushin delivered the infirmary ration – but disappeared from the catering block that very moment. Some force shoved him out into the yard, which was empty and quiet without any soldiers, and he wandered into the garden, where the earth was breathing coolly under its thick covering of grass. After about ten steps he came up against a concrete wall. The free branches of the garden flew on over it, as if the garden was growing on the edge of a precipice, but it wasn't the yard or the little garden that was broken off here by the wall – it was the Tashkent escort regiment. Since he couldn't walk any further, he lay down by that wall in the coolness, on the grass, in the shady twilight, and fell asleep.

The little Uzbek missed him at the catering block and set out to look for him, but didn't find him. Then, from midday onwards, the little Uzbek started concealing what had happened, keeping quiet, because he knew the Russian had gone missing. He did the ferrying work himself. He finished off the day, setting the catering block in perfect, gleaming order, like after a murder. He didn't leave the catering block again for anything . . . And suddenly Matiushin showed up. The little Uzbek looked at him with a dark, smouldering fire in his glance, but eyes fastened expectantly on Matiushin. The little Uzbek was beginning to understand, to feel something, numbly and submissively; he was probably suffering the torment of withdrawal. Matiushin took the plain plastic bag from under the cook's stove and shook it out into a small vat full of swill.

The cook huddled up quietly into a ball, as if the grass hadn't drowned in the leftovers of food and drink, but in his petty little soul.

Looking at him, Matiushin felt a light tremor of disaster, as if he could hear the booming of heavy footsteps drawing closer and closer, boots tramping, tramping – but he wasn't afraid. As if he had stopped believing in death, and in life. Let them kill him, so what . . . They'd come and they'd kill him. The little Uzbek trembled, lying on the floor, doubled up. Putting his arms round him without speaking, as if the cook was his brother, Matiushin fell asleep. The dirty yellow light burned until morning in the catering block, seeping down soundlessly from the ceiling, like gas. Matiushin kept waking up in a sweat, opening his eyes and seeing that pitiless, blinding light all around him, but then falling asleep again, feeling the firm bundle of human warmth close beside him.

PART THREE

When he opened his eyes the foreman was standing over him, towering up in the hungry air of the bright morning, freshly washed, with his slicked-back hair still wet.

'Now up you get quietly. You won't be back here again . . . '

The foreman led him away as if he was under armed escort.

In the empty ward – at this time everyone was waiting in the little garden to be called for feeding – Matiushin stripped the leaden grey sheets off his bed and raked them together into an armload. They went to the stores; there he returned everything that was the infirmary's and was given his own clothes, the ones in which he had been brought from Dorbaz. And they went out onto the hot, dusty porch, already baking in the sun.

'Walk on, walk on!' said the foreman, pushing him in the back, and he called another soldier who was standing not far away, as good as new, saying goodbye to someone. 'Hey, soldier boy, whatever your name is, the jaundice case! The date's over, follow me!' And as he waddled down the steps from the porch, he called to the others who'd been left behind: 'If anyone asks, tell them he's gone to staff HQ!'

Matiushin marched along, dragging his useless boots like wooden stocks. He had sewn up the tops slit open by the military doctor at Dorbaz some time during the last few days – he didn't remember when, it seemed like a dream. With their ugly seams of string, the boots looked like wounded living things, like toads hopping forward every time he took a step.

At staff HQ, a building that looked like a school, he heard his name shouted out and only then spotted the handful of soldiers sprawling back on a bench as if they were pinned down by his shadow.

'Matiushin! Well, don't just stand there! Don't say you don't recognise me!'

A skinny soldier got up off the bench and came over to him, grinning.

'Well, God's sent me a fine home-town buddy, blind and deaf! Well hi there, home-town buddy! Turned all stuck-up, have you?'

'He's famous for that . . . ' the jaundice case chipped in; he had appeared on the bench, looking pleased with himself. 'We were dying on the floor while he was in the mess, warming up the lunches.'

'The fools always die first,' the skinny one said with a smirk. 'So die, if you're a fool. Am I right, brothers? I was all right in the hospital. I wasn't dying either.'

And from that smirk, not entirely open, a little canny, Matiushin suddenly spotted that this was Rebrov, somehow grown old. 'So here we are . . . I knew we were going to serve together, and you're no fool, that's for sure! It was great the way you got away from the Moldavian . . . And the boots, those boots you're wearing, talk about boots!'

The discovery that they had ended up in the same time and place again was equally painful to both of them, although Rebrov had pretended he was glad to see his home-town buddy. The others carried on sitting there in a row without talking, but now Matiushin recognised them for himself, realising that he knew them too – they had been at Dorbaz.

'They took us from the hospital, so they must have taken you from the infirmary. Maybe you know where they're sending us?' Rebrov asked insistently. 'We had six men die in one week at Dorbaz; they say it was some kind of poisoning. They wouldn't stop hassling us, they were getting us up in the middle of the night – and off you go for a check-up, like it was some kind of interrogation! But what have you heard? The way I read things, they could have something important in store for us. If staff HQ's involved, I reckon they won't just ship us out to some company.'

'You wanted to be a sergeant . . . '

'I did, but I stopped wanting. I got sick of eating dirty fruit.'

At that moment the foreman emerged from the staff HQ and bawled:

'Everybody from quarantine, follow me!'

It was clean and cool in staff HQ. Suddenly awkward and timid, the foreman waited for permission to enter a ground-floor room, which turned out to be beautiful, filled with light paper rustlings and somehow blindingly naked because of the women sitting in it. Matiushin caught his breath at the warm, spicy scent of their perfume. They were sitting everywhere, behind desks, swallowed up to their necks by army shirts, as if sucked into the mire of a swamp, with only their small round heads, made light and airy by their hair-dos, bobbing up on the surface. A major was sitting among them forlornly. He wasn't speaking, yet somehow he managed to produce so much noise with his silence – running his hands over the desk and turning round so that his chair cracked, puffing and blowing, wheezing – that he had actually broken into a heavy sweat.

'Permission to enter?' asked the foreman.

'Granted,' the major growled, and when the foreman had scurried off, he turned, blushing crimson in shame, to the oldest of the women and said: 'Please begin.'

The woman sitting beside the safe started calling the men up to her by name and giving out money; she took a long time counting everything right down to the last kopeck and then made them sign for it, communicating with gestures, as if she was dumb.

While they were in that queue the realisation struck that they were being issued their first pay – and that meant they had served a month. The midday haze had a breath of freedom to it and, as they strolled on through the regimental base, they collected lots of tinned food, rusks and even sweets, and every one of them carried a cardboard box rattling with treats in his hands. Afterwards they were taken to the *chaikhana* and everyone was ordered to buy themselves water. In the *chaikhana* they cast ravening glances at the lemonade, thrusting all their money into the dumbfounded serving woman's hands like men in a trance. She was so frightened, she called the officers. They told the men to pay a rouble each, and that way the lemonade was bought with everyone chipping in. But after walking past the staff HQ building, they were surprised to reach a dreary, dusty ambulance into which they were ordered to load the boxes and then themselves. No one moved from the spot. Rebrov was the only one to speak up, with a hungry, ruthless kind of look.

'Lemonade, marmalade. . . Are they sending us back, then? Or somewhere even worse? That's just great!' he hissed though his teeth, sobering up and gazing round at everyone determinedly, as if figuring out who here was a survivor and who wasn't, who'd be surplus to requirements.

While they stood there like strangers, the unusual boxes of dry rations started attracting attention and inviting disaster: some soldiers crept up to the ambulance. Seeing that there weren't any officers, they peered into a box as if they owned it. Rebrov, worried about his lemonade, spoke up to frighten them off:

'Those are our commander's boxes. Don't touch them, lads, he'll be here any moment!'

The soldiers froze. They raised their goggle-eyed faces from the ground and gave him a long, gloomy look, but said nothing . . . When the regimental soldiers shambled off, Rebrov ordered the others to load the boxes into the ambulance and they jumped to obey him, then clambered into the back themselves – and hid. Then an officer appeared out of the staff HQ building and was delighted by the good order, but he read out two names and pulled two men out – they were Rebrov and the jaundice case – and led them back into the staff HQ. The back of the ambulance went quiet. Matiushin waited moment by moment for the rest of them to be set free, at least one at a time. For some reason he had the idea that when Rebrov and the jaundice case were let out, they had been rescued. But suddenly Rebrov stuck his head into the back of the ambulance and shouted:

'Let's go, brothers. Goodbye, Tashkent!'

As they raced through the warm, bright, white city with its clay-stove houses drowning in flowers and greenery as if they were mid-winter snow, they remembered the jaundice case who had been as delighted by his good luck as if it was sunshine, but he'd been left behind, he'd vanished inside staff HQ, and they had his lemonade now. On the platform at the railway station, which they reached riding like the wind, the group lined up one man at a time and Matiushin could see them all clearly. There was the same number as fingers on a hand, his brain made the calculation automatically: six deadbeats, including him. On the way to the station Rebrov had insisted again that they were being sent for training as cooks; supposedly he'd heard in staff HQ that their team would be taken to Kazakhstan and he'd figured out the bit about training as cooks for himself. If they were sending them off that far and weren't worried about the cost, it meant this was serious business, they were being taken for training, and what could men like them be trained as, after being ill, except as cooks, there weren't any specialists among them, were there – he questioned everyone briskly about that – and no electricians or signals men either. Rebrov strained, he tried really hard, giving neither himself nor the others a moment's rest. He hardly even knew the men with whom he had been collected from the Tashkent Military Hospital that morning, and now he was hastily trying to win them over, ignoring only Matiushin, who kept to himself.

Soon the platform was completely flooded with local folk, but the soldiers didn't drown in that sea, they stood there like an island. When the train arrived it was scarcely moving, and then the people, old and young alike, flowed into the gaping throats of the carriages in refreshing rivulets. The clamorous bustle of humanity – that was all that remained in Matiushin's soul at the end of this unbelievable time he had lived through. Children's shrieks, strident abuse and the barking of hoarse-voiced conductors engendered in Matiushin's soul a solitary sense of an ending, but it wasn't like a death to him; it flooded through his chest as warmth, it lulled him with the simple sadness of travelling.

It was a sitting carriage: hard wooden seats without even any mattresses, though the carriage was crammed full with people. The adroit conductor seated families on a single seat. Almost everyone there had no ticket, so he swore at them army-style at the top of his voice, aware of his power, and still somehow managed to feel compassion for these people and help them. Half-naked but wearing his strict peaked cap, thoroughly saturated with smoke, as guileful as a snake, with a throat hoarse from drink, he yelled and understood in various different languages, as if he had as many heads and souls. His job was to tamp down the contents of the ticketless carriage. And the conductor hurtled around the motionless carriage, as if they weren't standing dozily at the platform but rolling down a steep embankment.

When the train started and they were off, almost immediately they stripped to their shorts in the unbearable swelter and drank hot lemonade. They travelled without speaking until the small stations started flickering by. The train would suddenly stop and stand quietly for long up, like a fish, was cold and dumb, pleasantly rounded. Yelsk, Penza, Tashkent, this Tselinograd. Northwards, he thought exultantly, homewards – and the fish didn't flap about, it gazed one-eyed, like a map. His human brain, half-stupefied with joy, held at least half the world at that moment. As if it was drunk, this half-of-the-world vaporised the time and Matiushin set off to wander round the carriage. He drifted out into the vestibule. Two marvellous, anonymous young sailors were standing there smoking, with identical attaché cases at their feet. Their faces were hidden in clouds of tobacco smoke. Matiushin was entranced by the way they were identically doubled, like in a mirror, so he staggered quietly into the corner and lit up a cigarette – only because these two were smoking. They conspired about something incomprehensible, discussed something, taking no notice at all of the stranger. Matiushin looked out from his corner at the young sailors, and soon the hammering of the wheels started sounding duller and duller and he imagined he was hearing the booming of the sea. Although he had never seen the sea in his life, he fancied that their carriage was swaying on the waves as it sailed along. But stretching out on all sides for many hundreds of kilometres there was nothing except an expanse of cold desert. The sailors seemed to have appeared in this dry land from somewhere high above it. And then there was another miracle: he recognised those stocky, sturdy young sailors with high cheekbones as two inhabitants of the steppe, as alike as twins, and he couldn't tell if they were Kirghiz or Kazakhs . . . The train slowed down and a station approached. A bright beam from the floodlights lanced into the vestibule – and on the young sailors' foreheads, on their round caps, the wrought-silver letters of some fleet glinted brightly. Instantly they themselves flared up in the blinding beam of light, taut and white in their sailors' shirts, and then the vestibule was plunged into the dark of night, and they stood there charred black for a minute until the light lashed at them again. Through the window the full extent of the junction was visible, lit up by a floodlight: a grey field glinting with a fine dew of rails and herds of goods trains, standing like bulls, motionless and unattended. They were clustered together, waiting, like at a slaughterhouse. The train moved slower and slower, the carriages crept along as if on tiptoe towards the station, across this grey field. They stopped at a platform silver with dust, as if covered with snow in the night, and now there was time to for them to catch their breath. A man ran across the earth, scurried across it like a lizard. A woman's mournful voice hooted like an owl over the station speakers, giving someone orders, and then the woman summoned unknown people out of the blank air and quarrelled with them and they yelled. The little station, entirely white, radiated an aura of mute peace. Matiushin saw the name of this place where they had arrived, spelled out on a building in letters the height of a man, embracing each other on the roof of the little station, looking like the anonymous sailors: CHU. The

window. The desert halts, although they were brief, even
hasty, filled him with a dreary terror. Every stop seemed
like the last to Matiushin.

Suddenly a tramping of feet, howls of joy and a
concerted human droning erupted out of nowhere and
scattered the dismal phantom of the night. He twisted
round like a little animal and pressed his face against the
window. In the circle of light hovering beside the carriage,
a whole crowd of folk had gathered. Laughing faces with
slanting eyes flickering like lights and mouths like slits
of joy; shadows danced with wide-flung legs and strong,
resonant voices sang. Men with whips, women, children,
even horses held by the bridle off at one side, all swirled
about beside the carriage. Two patches of snowy white
drowned in the embraces of indistinguishable shabby
outfits. Held shoulder-high, the sailors were dragged into
the circle, and people crushed up against each other just
in order to touch them. The sailors bobbed and pranced
about, floating on people's backs, clutching their peak-
less caps so they wouldn't be torn off their heads. And
with their other hands they clutched their fragile-looking
attaché cases, waving them in the air like flags. Those two
flags jerked about for a long time, jutting above the crowd,
before they were lowered to the ground. The sailors were
carried to the horses and set down. They climbed onto the
horses with ponderous dignity, making their mounts sag
under them like frail little boats, and were intoxicated
to find themselves way up above the ground, swaying in

the saddles. People around them started whooping, either egging them on or expressing admiration, gazing at the flat, thin bread cakes of their caps with the ribbons and golden letters, and at the small, bony, flattened objects that they were holding in their hands like bags. In the night the faces couldn't be made out, but they all seemed somehow dear and beautiful to Matiushin. To demonstrate their boldness to their relatives and the sailors, little kids who looked like small midges launched into a gallop, clutching on tight to the shaggy manes of their horses. Black herds of them hurtled along the line of carriages. As they flew past, they flogged the carriage with their whips, lashing at its blind, sleeping windows as if they were eyes, which Matiushin found bizarre to see – but even so they couldn't wake anyone up. The carriages were as silent as lifeless barrels, which was probably why the kids dared to whip them. Soon the crowd of folk flooded back from Matiushin's carriage and all took their seats as if taking up their posts for action. The men moved aside slightly and each of them drew himself erect on his own steed. The women and children sat two or even three together on broad-backed, bloated nags, ready to set off after the men. The sailors were imperious, radiating a new, mysterious strength. Already accustomed to this strength of theirs, they sat enthroned, choosing to keep their lips calmly closed and say nothing.

Happy at not having to wait for the train any longer and tired after this nocturnal raid, the entire horde stood in the darkness of the way station, and their horses could be heard stamping their feet, murmuring restlessly and breathing out clouds of steam, as if they were smoking.

When the train set off, the horsemen also moved off quietly, level with the carriages. The train picked up speed, but the people on the horses picked up speed too, not falling back but racing after it – then suddenly went dashing off into nowhere, into the blackness, and disappeared from sight. For a long time Matiushin fancied that the horsemen were still close, but time began flowing more drowsily. He got tired of waiting and moved away from the window.

That night, way station after way station, their carriage emptied of people. After Balkhash, where they woke with the morning, when the soldiers roused each other they saw a half-empty carriage. They were moving faster, although there were just as many senseless stops. They knew they were supposed to arrive by midnight at some place called Karaganda, but in the midst of the cold, grey steppe morning it began to seem as if the sky was darkening and midnight was already approaching, the moment you simply thought about it. During the doldrums of the rest of the journey, the companions in good fortune dreamed until darkness came that they were being taken to train as cooks. One was a half-Czech from Syzran, a tailor by the name of Husak, small but with huge eyes, as if he was crying, and a leg that was crooked from birth – Matiushin remembered the funny way he had walked across the platform at Tashkent, dragging his leg the way a mother drags a stubborn kid along after her. There was a quiet one too, with poor eyesight, the kind of person who likes to study. His name was Sergei and he said he was from a music college. There were Anikin and Kulagin, as alike as two brothers after the hepatitis, two fellow townsmen from Penza; one of them had been a landscape gardener in his previous life, the other hadn't had time to do anything since school. Matiushin felt depressed: they thought they were all going to be trained and turned into cooks, but he didn't want to be a cook. He didn't even want to share his air with them on the journey – he'd been choking on his melancholy since the end of the first day. The lights of the main station glittered malevolently that midnight, at the hour of their arrival. They disembarked from the half-empty carriage in Karaganda and immediately saw the gun-mount backside of an army truck jutting out of the darkness. The wind was bending small trees that were swamp-coloured in the night, and the damp air had the smell of a swamp. It seemed as if Karaganda was always like this: chained to greyness, cold and damp. As they waited to learn their fate they froze in the cold and wind on a platform as black as if it was wet. After the joy of boundless light and warmth, they felt as if now they had ended up in a damp, cold basement – not on the ground, but under it.

*

Keeping the men in the cold beside the truck, the duty officer swore and insisted stubbornly that he had nothing to feed them and nowhere to put them, and things had to be decided somehow. The hope flared up for a moment that they were here by mistake, but the escorting officer from the Tashkent regiment squelched it. He swore and insisted even more stubbornly than the duty officer. It became clear who was going to win. The strong man got what he wanted, the weak man's faith failed him and he backed down – and beds were found in the middle of the night. In the darkness, they guessed from the smell that it was some kind of infirmary again.

Early in the morning, between four and five, they were woken by local men who had heard the noise in the night and come to gape. Outside the window, rain flailed about in the wind. A large pan of yesterday's meat and cabbage soup was dragged in for them and even cold it tasted good; they were more generous with food here than in Tashkent. The new arrivals discovered that they had ended up in an escort regiment where men served as soldiers, and didn't learn to be cooks. They couldn't make any sense of why they had been sent from the escort regiment in Tashkent to this one. In the morning some majors came into the room, looked at the men without speaking, as if they were sick, infectious animals, and went away again. The men didn't go anywhere else all day long. Starting from the next morning, they were driven round the rain-soaked town to various hospitals: in one they had blood samples, in another they had their stomachs palped. They were brought back to the infirmary, fed lunch, then taken back to the doctors to be examined.

Then Husak was separated out and taken away, and he didn't come back. Anikin and Kulagin disappeared, taken away to a barracks for the night. Nobody wanted to explain anything.

The next day it seemed as if they'd come for the rest of the men, who were ordered outside. The little hills of hangars and warehouses stretched out in lines behind barbed wire as they wandered along the edge of the road after a little officer. At one warehouse, where a van was standing idle and silent with its doors wide open, revealing that it was stuffed with large-headed pigs' carcasses, the officer stuck his head into a low little door.

'Glebich, I've brought some manpower.'

'Oo-oo-oo . . . ' The approving drone floated out of depths into which an iron staircase led down, and when they walked down it, they found themselves in a cold stone cellar, fragrant with the aroma of fried meat. A dishevelled, softhearted-looking man was frying the meat for himself on a stove, as if he were working a miracle.

'Eating it straight away?' the little officer asked ingratiatingly.

'I'm taking a sample! And who are these? Where'd you drag them in from?'

'Why, they're from the infirmary, let them work . . . '

'From the infirmary . . . Well right enough, work's a healer. Now then, my sons, you saw those dead pigs. They won't get you dirty, don't worry; the important thing is, make sure you don't drop them: meat's treacherous stuff. Drop it and it'll start stinking.'

After an hour's work, pork from the carcasses that had been taciturnly weighed and hoisted up under the ceiling was browning and sputtering away without any smoke. The smell given off while it fried put the warehouseman in a mellow mood; after eating a bit, he flourished his cleaver and threw another great chunk into the frying pan, unafraid of any germs, and when the soldiers had done the job, he gave each one of them a piece like a slice of bread. True, the little officer refused fastidiously, but he was angry looking at the fry-up and the way they tucked into it. The warehouseman relaxed and encouraged them:

'Eat up, eat up! You're people too, you need your vitamins too.'

'And what about us?' the little officer asked boldly. 'I'll wait and drop in when it's a bit darker, but don't you do me down, Glebich.'

'I won't do you down . . . These are good lads, handy, bring them again. I'm tired of running around begging.'

'You couldn't beg snow in winter from our lot, the kind of people we've got now.'

'No, it's the way times are – got to keep a tight rein on things. But I could do with a soldier to help out, one at least . . . Are these all sick then?'

'It's time for this lot to die! They've been dumped on us from Tashkent, it got too hot for them there,' the little officer said with a grin. 'But just look at them, they work as if they were alive. Run over to our chief, maybe he'll fix it up, and then take them, or they'll be sent off to the fucking companies; they're short of men in the companies.'

The warehouseman looked all three of them over and nodded at Matiushin:

'What's your name? Like to join me here in the stores?'

'No, I'll go with all the rest, we're off back to Tashkent.'

'Why, you're a fool, lad – look, he doesn't want to go to heaven!' the warehouseman laughed. 'Who's going to ask him where he wants to go!'

The little officer took them back stealthily to the infirmary. When they were ensconced in the ward, Rebrov started hurling reproaches at Matiushin:

'What Tashkent, who's this you're going with? You bastard, you should have told him, you ought to have spoken up for all of us, said we wanted him to take us all. You heard him, they haven't got any men!'

Matiushin slumped against the wall and stared silently, as if afraid of starting a fight, but Rebrov was furious. He fell silent of his own accord, ran out of steam. That evening the one who could play the trumpet, the third one, couldn't take any more and decided to risk it: he'd found out from local men that they were fond of music in this regiment and there was a club where they played their trumpets, and he ran off to the club. And *he* didn't come back again either. But a truck that looked like a bread van with iron sides came for the rest of the men. Matiushin had never seen one like it before. He realised they were being taken away for ever, and he felt sick at the sight of Rebrov and his repulsive face: that interminable, despicable wish of his, for them to be together, had come true. Rebrov himself was shattered. A tired-looking soldier and officer were having a smoke by the truck.

'Fucking hell, Karpovich!' the soldier said with a smile, as if he'd recognised someone he knew, keeping his fastidious little eyes fixed on Matiushin.

'Shut it, you foreign devil, you. Stop fuddling my lads' brains, gawping like that!' the genial officer rapped out. 'Right, climb in, let's go. The cons have been loaded up, we'll drive like the wind. If you've got fags, ok, smoke, only the butts go out the window. Our driver's a strict one, no littering in the cabin. And we'll have a proper heart-to-heart at home. Ours is a fine place, lads, like being out in the country.'

They climbed into the iron lobby of this slammer on wheels. The entire back of it was taken up with two cages divided by a partition and locked shut; there was something living lurking in them, making low grumbling sounds. Matiushin was struck by – not a stench exactly, but a fusty, earthy smell, like from a greenhouse. The soldier slammed the door shut behind them and walked away. There was a smell of hunger and pain. They heard gates rattling – the van drove out and the back of it started swaying about and screeching, clattering the cages. Rebrov sat in his corner with a haunted look, not saying a word. Matiushin clambered over to the window and breathed in the fresh wind. First they were run around through the town for a little bit, and then driven into the gloomy, frozen steppe and dragged on across it.

They would have gone for each other's throats, but they'd run out of strength ages ago. They held out until a stumpy little railway station flashed by in the window and there was a whiff of soot from a railway line and a glimpse of the chipped wooden boards of houses or sheds – they couldn't make out which in the damp, smoky, cotton-wool air. A minute later the truck sputtered into silence. A soldier swung the door open and stood to one side, as if he was used to it, dangling his automatic rifle in his hand.

They climbed out at a neat, tidy barracks that looked like a residential block. About three hundred metres away, a sheer, high, long, dirty white wall soared upwards, as if it was patching a hole in the sky. There were nesting boxes on its naked apexes, and they could see the little fledgling sentries. The sentries watched from on high as the truck drove inside and dropped off two unknown men – they waved their arms and shouted. There was a distant hoot from the station. The roofs of a village stood, hunched over, out in the steppe. A welcoming little family of soldiers darted out of the domestic-looking barracks to surround and greet the new arrivals. All the soldiers looked the same and they all gaped at Matiushin and laughed, their eyes flashing and twinkling:

'A new Karpovich has arrived! Karpovich's brother! Karpovich's brother has arrived!'

The genial officer, the elderly, grey-haired man who had driven them from Karaganda in the prison truck, was the sergeant-major here; Matiushin heard his name – Pomogalov.

Pomogalov sat in a separate room, the orderly room, with its doors standing wide open, and fell asleep like a log at his desk. Everyone who was in the barracks whiled away the time until lights-out in the recreation room. Matiushin remembered the name of one of the soldiers, Dybenko, and the story that he, or some other soldier, told about a girl being raped in some town or other. Dybenko presided in the recreation room, apparently in charge there. He sat in the middle, half-naked, stout and ponderous. In the meantime, his trousers were being ironed for him by a ginger-haired soldier with whom he spoke like an equal, to show the others that he wasn't humiliating the soldier, simply training him. Apart from the incomprehensible exclamations when they arrived, the new arrivals in the company were given the silent treatment. Rebrov tried to break into the general conversation, but they listened to him without saying anything and looked away.

As the soldiers trickled out of the recreation room

Oleg Pavlov

Dybenko started talking. He turned lazily towards Matiushin, nodded at his uncovered shoulder, where he had
spotted the tattoo, and asked:

'What's the idea, suicide boy? In the correctional zone
you get killed for a tattoo like that.'

'Why don't you just piss off!' Matiushin swore without
even thinking, sick and tired of all this uncertainty and
of being examined.

'Well, sorry,' Dybenko said awkwardly. 'But round here
we don't wear designs like that, you need to understand,
whatever your human name is, if you have one.'

Matiushin came to his senses and told him his name.

'Well, since you're Vasilii, let's talk. I'm Vasilii too.
But don't go dropping any more clangers like that. This is
the zone. You answer for what you say here. Once you've
said it, consider it done. You take a life or else . . . you
have yours taken.'

He was half-frowning, half-smiling. He gave Matiushin
a needle and a razor, without the slightest sign of squeam-
ishness, and spoke in an ordinary voice, no longer guilty.

'Help yourself, no charge, suicide boy, but spoil what's
mine and you have to give me back two like it or die. If
you've borrowed something, know what the payback is.'

The dormitory wasn't a barracks either but a large
hall. There were more empty beds than Matiushin could
count. The men slept on whichever they liked, wherever they liked, but he already knew that the empty
beds belonged to men on twenty-four-hour guard duty

in the zone. Tomorrow the men here would go off to the zone, merely exchanging glances with the others at the change of guard. He took a bed in an alcove next to Dybenko, who called Matiushin over, questioned him to his heart's content in the darkness and cheerfully told Matiushin all about himself. Dybenko turned out to be a yearling sergeant who had been demoted and exiled from his regiment because when he was drunk in an attic somewhere he'd flung the macaroni that he was eating with his vodka at a portrait of Brezhnev . . . When Dybenko got tired, he started falling asleep, and Matiushin only just remembered in time to ask why he'd had those exclamations about some Karpovich or other shouted in his face.

'A-a-ah . . . We've got this screwball here . . . Keep well away from him, or he'll pollute you too . . . ' Dybenko replied sleepily.

Morning came. An officer appeared in the barracks – young, swarthy-skinned, supple: he walked past the soldiers, not letting them near him, disdaining them. The officer watched everyone in silence. The hall filled up with movement, like a fermenting tub. Drunk on their own drowsiness, the men all walked in the same direction, all did the same thing. In the yard, after they'd jostled their way outside, semi-naked, the cold bit into their skin, and it jerked Matiushin awake like pain. The great, dirty-white wall was still standing there, frozen motionless in the steppe, stony hard in the damp air. On one watchtower there was the black figure of a sentry wrapped in a cloak tent, but the towers further off disappeared into the mist, which was like clouds that had wandered down from the sky.

After the usual morning bustle and an almost home-style breakfast in a half-empty mess the size of an ordinary room, with little flowers painted on its walls that gave off a sharp smell of oil paint in the warmth, the time after reveille was abruptly cut short. The soldiers left to go to work: from their well-fed mutterings Matiushin realised that they were going to the zone. But the new arrivals were separated off and stayed with the soldier who was on orderly duty in the silent barracks, abandoned by everyone. They weren't told what to do. So now they were like orderlies too, with no place of their own in all this empty space. Then the officer, who had also stayed in the barracks, called them in to his office one at a time.

The officer sat at a desk, and Matiushin sat on a stool facing the officer. Sitting inside these four walls, the officer seemed either lonely or very haughty. He asked a series of apparently simple questions, wanting to hear something about Matiushin's family and his past, but in reply Matiushin only complained stubbornly that he had ended up in this regiment by mistake and he ought to be sent back to Tashkent. He'd spent less than twenty-four hours in this new company but, after the way they'd called him by someone else's name, jabbing their fingers at him as if he was a freak, he felt so lonely here that he was having dismal thoughts about himself. Probably this first acquaintance aroused a feeling of aversion in the handsome, manly officer; as he let Matiushin out of his office, the officer looked straight through him. Matiushin was aware that he hadn't been any help, and he walked out indifferently, as if he was sinking down under water. He was only surprised by the man's surname – Arman – and the fact that he turned out to be the company's deputy commander for political affairs at such a young age.

The soldiers came back tired from their work and they looked more cantankerous over lunch. One barked out that those who hadn't been working should only take the black bread; they weren't supposed to eat the wheat bread. After lunch, lights-out was suddenly announced: they were supposed to sleep in the middle of the day. For Matiushin, getting into bed felt a bit bizarre, like packing himself into a box. Weary, the soldiers fell asleep one by one and then, after reveille, between five and six, they got ready for the zone.

The weapons room looked like a cage, with a row of thick metal bars instead of one wall. It was right there, deep inside the sleeping area. The soldiers walked through the hall, with its rows of empty beds, already armed. Their automatic rifles were black, with battered wooden facings on their stocks. The empty beds and black automatics filled Matiushin's eyes, crowding out the men. The genial sergeant-major from the day before,

Pomogalov, went off to the zone, in charge. A little girl, his daughter, had come to the barracks with him from the village, muffled up in a winter scarf. She held on tight to her father, which amused the soldiers, but she wasn't afraid of them at all. The sergeant-major managed to be affectionate with his little daughter and shout at the soldiers as well. The soldiers strode off along the road to the zone, respectfully slowing their step for their commander's tiny daughter, who slithered her little feet over the dirt behind her father.

After some time, the platoon coming off duty from the zone appeared on the road. They burst into the yard with their automatics and scattered. In an instant the yard was like a meadow covered with faces instead of grass and blossoming with non-Russian speech. Some, gasping and swaying, ran clumsily behind the barracks. Others disappeared into the barracks or dashed to fraternise with the mellow, well-fed day orderly and grab his delicious cigarettes. Matiushin and Rebrov now became part of this platoon; they merged into it and milled about in the yard, as if they were with everybody else.

'Karpovich, there's your brother,' cheerful voices called out in delight. It was the non-Russians standing to one side who were shouting. They watched and waited, urging on someone who couldn't be made out amid the motley rabble. Matiushin stared into that rabble, searching for someone who looked like him, but out came a smiling, thick-lipped, round-faced man – the very picture of a cook. He flung his big arms out, as if he had been pining wearily for a long time, and grabbed Matiushin, bear-hugging him at speed.

'Greetings, brother, I've heard about you,' he sang out in front of everybody. 'I've been waiting impatiently to say hello. How have you settled in? How are you getting on?'

The men around them chortled and guffawed. They were laughing at the soldier, because he spoke so loudly and mawkishly. They were amused by the way he toadied to Matiushin, who glared at him with a mixture of anger and detachment.

Matiushin remembered very well what Dybenko had said in the night, but this wasn't the man he had been expecting as he grew less rational and angrier during the day. This man was pitiful in the way he tried to please, but had the strength of patience and was big, solid and strong in general.

Another two men entered the yard from the road on their own – a titchy little pigeon-toed sergeant and a solemn, severe soldier, leading an equally severe-looking Alsatian at his heels; the dog was swinging its head around briskly in its collar, drawn towards the men. They were walking on past, but the soldier looked round and shouted:

'Karpovich! Follow me!'

The mass of soldiers fell dismally silent. The yard was suddenly calm.

'Come on, don't forget about your friend,' the soldier said with a smile and added rapidly: 'Come the evening, we'll take a stroll well away from this lot, where it's a bit quieter. I'll enjoy it especially.'

Karpovich set off at a brisk run, overtook the two men, and the three of them disappeared round the corner of the barracks together. But there was a morbid floundering in that man, something downtrodden that made Matiushin feel sorry for him. That was the way people with a hernia moved – struggling, holding it with their hand. Matiushin caught a glimpse of flinty-looking seams on the tops of Karpovich's boots – exactly the same as the freaks that Matiushin was dragging about on his own feet. At some time Karpovich's boots had been slit open and then sewn up with either wire or string in exactly the same way. Matiushin realised that he had been recognised as this pitiful man's double because of his boots.

He stood there, the first in line, with Karpovich beside him, relieved to realise the truth. At supper they were seated by height again, beside each other. Karpovich nibbled on leaves of white bread like a caterpillar. The men laughed at him, the way they probably always did, but he ate his fill, enjoying it. Not everyone at the table ate white bread, only six or seven men from the entire platoon, and for some reason Karpovich had that right. In the barracks Matiushin asked Karpovich for a razor and a needle and thread. Everything required was found in an instant and Karpovich whispered:

'I sensed a kindred spirit immediately, let me tell you honestly. I've suffered more than my share too, but it hasn't got them anywhere, so don't let it get to you, little brother.'

Karpovich spoke as if he was being watched. Before lights out Matiushin gave back everything he had borrowed from him without a word. In this platoon the alcove where Matiushin and Dybenko had spent the night belonged to different men. Without a bed of his own, Matiushin was obliged to go back to Karpovich, who knew which beds were free. Everybody tried to huddle together and not sleep out in empty space. Matiushin spotted Rebrov running about, lackeying for someone. When it was already night Matiushin was woken by a loud voice that he didn't know. In the darkness he made out someone being roused from his bed and led away. Then he calmly fell asleep. Morning came. The same officer was striding round the barracks.

At the morning roll call Arman ordered Pomogalov to leave the new men in formation and they marched off with the rest of the platoon. As they were approaching the zone, the cold surface of the sky suddenly turned a bright, tremulous blue and the sun glittered brilliantly, reflected in that coldness as if it was water. They crowded into the echoing concrete box of a small yard, glancing sideways through the massive, wide-open door of the guardhouse, then marched in a line into a gap that opened up in the old camp fortifications, where there were beams and rusty iron piles sticking out and mountainous heaps of sand. When they were released from duty, the men sat down to smoke. The titchy sergeant – a Chinese – was in command. Allowing the other soldiers to do nothing, he took Matiushin and Rebrov and led them off to a bleak spot where the repair work ended and the sandy strip of the perimeter security zone, overgrown with tufts of weeds, stretched off wearily into the distance. He walked about for a while with his clever little face wrinkled up, sighed a bit, scrunched the sand underfoot and ordered them to clear the security strip of tufts of grass.

Matiushin wandered along the walls, kicking out the tufts with his boot. Rebrov scrabbled in the sand, making an effort, working, moving forward and, although he wanted to seem independent, he soon lost patience and shouted:

'Come and work, you bastard! And quick! I don't want to lose people's respect here because of you! I respect myself.'

They clashed with a dull thud, fell and rolled in the sandy soil, scrabbling and trying to choke each other. A sentry spotted them fighting from his watchtower and called the Chinese from the reinforcement works. He came running, panting hard, with a piece of wire that he'd picked up on the way, and when he reached them he immediately lashed out without speaking. That whistling wire burned more viciously than fire. They jumped up at his first swing, but the Chinese started circling round menacingly and lashing at them, giving them no chance to gather their wits. The blinding pain spun them round and set them running. The Chinese kept up with them, driving them all the way to the end, where the band of soldiers greeted them with loud horse laughs.

Matiushin whiled away the rest of the working time with Karpovich, smoking at his expense. They set an iron pile in the ground where Karpovich had already dug a pit, working on his own, and for the first time in his life Matiushin saw a real live convict. A team of them, welders, were led out to the repairs. They welded hooks onto the ready piles. There were showers of fiery sparks and glimpses of the convicts' lean, stringy bodies as they moved out from behind the sparks and then back in under the bright rain. Suddenly one of them dived out from under the fiery shower. He slung an armful of the iron rods he needed onto his shoulder and set off, slowed by the weight. For about ten steps he smiled, looking at Matiushin – the new, unfamiliar soldier who was standing in his way. But the only thing Matiushin made out was that all his teeth were metal, and then – without even remembering the face, because the convict was sweeping past him in a tight, living bundle of sinew and muscle – he saw the tattoo on the man's chest: devils being boiled in a cauldron. For just an instant Matiushin fancied that those devils were alive. As the convict stepped out, the devils in the cauldron twitched and squirmed about. Sensing that the soldier was eyeing him, the convict rasped out audaciously:

'Move aside! Make way!'

After lunch and a sleep this platoon went off to the zone and the other one, with Dybenko, came back. He and Matiushin met like old buddies and embraced. The guards in this prison-camp platoon embraced as if they were kissing – they shook hands, took the other man's shoulder with their free hand and pressed their cheeks together.

A day later Matiushin ended up working under Dybenko's watch tower. Dybenko spent his watch on the tower as if he was the boss. He took a stout board out from under the roof of his little kennel, arranged it crosswise and sat on it with his back held straight, so it looked like he was standing. Occasionally throwing a word down to Matiushin pottering about in the perimeter security zone, he would suddenly strike up a conversation with someone out of sight, looking straight ahead, over into the zone. Sitting in the pit between the fences, Matiushin could hear the voices. A twisted rag bundle flew up over the camp wall towards the tower. But it didn't flop down loosely: its load must have been heavy – and Dybenko caught it.

'All right, get on with it!' he shouted to someone when he'd emptied the rag, and turned his head back towards freedom.

A khaki-coloured sack went flying over into the zone, and then another one.

'And you stop gawking, it's too soon for you yet!' Dybenko growled to Matiushin, spotting that the soldier had frozen below the tower and was watching.

Beyond the tower, the invisible railway station droned and clattered. The local trains howled like hysterical bitches, right on schedule. Dybenko said nothing while he thought, gazing into the zone like a statue, and then he came to life.

'Listen, there's no one around, run over to the shop in the station and get some bagels. You're the suicide soldier. Come on, pay back your debt! Don't get the wind up, you're not the first, it's been done before. Get up this wall!'

The camp wall was like a raft battened tight against the sky. Dybenko encouraged him offhandedly in the climb, indifferent to anything that might happen apart from the bagels. He handed Matiushin a paper rouble that he'd just earned, curled into a trough in his fingers, and pointed to a squat, grubby little house at the station, with a heap of coal lying abandoned beside it under the open sky and strange, spindly trees growing skywards. Matiushin, already sitting on the fence, glanced around fitfully, didn't see any men in shoulder straps in all that open space – and jumped down into the tall wild grass that grew outside the camp.

In the shop they weren't surprised to see the soldier. Women were standing in a queue. Boorish cockroaches were running across the floorboards. A cat was dozing right there on the counter – he must have been the languid, aged serving woman's favourite. Matiushin waited his turn in the queue, turning numb when the door swung open and banged shut behind him, and walked out, burying his dead hands in the fragrant muff of bagels. He ran quickly over the stretch of wasteland, stuffed his purchase into the front of his tunic and climbed back into the zone with even greater difficulty, his belly swollen out by the bagels.

It was July. Halfway through it the rain gave way to heat – but steppe heat, with free-ranging winds and shuddering cold at night. It turned out that the officers had all gone off on leave at the beginning of the month. The only ones left in the company were Arman and sergeant-major Pomogalov, whom the young political officer clearly didn't like.

Matiushin improved Arman's opinion of him, without even knowing it, at the rifle range. He could shoot, because he had often been allowed to amuse himself like that at his father's bases, where he was given either a pistol or an automatic rifle to blast away with. When he fired a gun for the first time, as a boy, he thought he'd gone deaf and for a long time he couldn't understand what had happened. Devastated by the sheer din, as if he were a metal barrel and the automatic had been fired at him, the next time he fired as if he had already learned from practice that an automatic rifle requires strength, but only as much strength as an ordinary meat mincer. So now at the rifle range he simply squeezed himself up tight against the butt, saw the targets, set the sight on each of them in his mind's eye and fired when the officer gave the command. All the targets were downed. Before the line-up, when the shooting was over, Arman praised him loudly. Then he suddenly walked over to one of the sergeants, a Tajik, ordered him to hand over his automatic, struck a pose, but didn't lie down, and fired off two full clips in rapid succession, mowing down the same targets with sheer sustained bursts of fire. The Tajik stood there without stirring a muscle, stony-faced. After his amusement, the political officer tossed the automatic that he didn't need any more into the man's hands. Back in the barracks, as the men cleaned their weapons, this sergeant flung his rifle, with its fouled barrel, down on the floor, and started weeping angrily in front of everyone, not embarrassed, and Matiushin heard him curse the young political officer through his teeth.

'Arman, may your mother croak, may your father croak . . . May your children croak . . . ' And then the Tajik resigned himself to what this man had done to him, to the pain he had caused him, and wiped the tears off his face.

That evening Pomogalov's platoon went off to the zone, but the political officer kept the sergeant-major in the company headquarters and appointed himself officer of the guard in his place. Every time Arman went out on guard duty was special and this time there were two new soldiers on duty. Nobody was pleased. Matiushin was given an automatic in the weapons room and he lined up with everybody else on the parade ground, but the news that they were going on duty with Arman made him feel coerced and guilty. The guardhouse was like a beehive. Even inside it everything seemed as though it was waxed and had the sweetish smell of some kind of myrrh.

Before the squad left for the zone Arman ordered everyone to be searched, as if they weren't marching off to guard convicts but were convicts themselves. It wasn't clear to Matiushin why they were frisked, after all they left the guardhouse just as they had been, except that now they were armed. He was put on 'number three', the third tower on the circle of the camp – a quiet, swampy spot, where there was a little factory. However, apart from the factory's swollen wall, Matiushin didn't see anything. The zone was boxed in by walls and couldn't be seen even from the tower. During the second shift when it was already night, the black swamp around the little factory greeted Matiushin with blank silence. He could see the fences by the lights, but all he could hear was the rustling whisper of the air. Because his hearing wasn't very good, he fancied there was something alive behind every shadow. And then he started imagining sounds as well – rushing movements in the night, knocking and footsteps.

After a while, although he didn't hear any steps, Matiushin saw two shadows on the squad path, already close to the tower, but after a moment he made out a peaked cap and realised that one of these men was Arman. Arman climbed up onto the tower in silence and made him explain why they hadn't been hailed as they approached, peering at him angrily, not believing that Matiushin had seen them and simply forgotten to shout. Matiushin served out his watch more dead than alive and went back to the guardhouse, tormented now by his deafness and afraid to tell anyone about it. But after that night he found himself in the guard officer's room, and Arman, continuing his night-time interrogation in the morning, wouldn't let him out. Matiushin was so tired and short of sleep that he could barely stay on his feet, so he told the truth without even thinking about it: that his deafness was to blame. The young political officer listened but, for some reason, he grimaced fastidiously, interrupted Matiushin mid-word and ordered him to leave.

After suffering through the full twenty-four hours of the watch with agonised endurance, Matiushin had come to terms with the previous night and regretted now that he had complained about his disability. As for Arman, whether he had forgotten about that twenty-four hours or not, the only sign he gave afterwards was to cast an occasional sidelong glance at Matiushin – and it seemed as if what was said in the guard officer's room was already a thing of the past.

The zone was painfully casting off its old skin and renewing itself. Major repairs were under way: stretches of the old wire-mesh fences were knocked down, together with their posts. Replacement wire was shipped in and lay about in tight steel rolls. Iron piles with hooks were being set up to replace the wooden pillars. After tearing the wooden beams off the old wire-mesh fences like bones out of a fish, the men started rolling them up, as if they were rolling large wire snowballs. They rolled up a path of wire three metres wide, and soon the prickly, rusty snowball was taller than a man. When they simply couldn't push it any more, they cut the ends of the wire and started all over again.

The convicts had to finish the welding work on the fortifications, and Matiushin had just been taken off the tower, he was free, so Pomogalov took him along. Pomogalov urged the convicts on, making them work, and Matiushin sat at the side with his automatic, keeping an eye on things. The sergeant-major sweated harder than the workers did and in the end he was genuinely delighted that they managed to get things done in time. The convicts had a foreman who hardly did any work but they all obeyed him – he lay there in the shadow under a tower, wrapped in a monkey jacket as if he were sick, and talked to the team. He asked the sergeant-major's permission to prepare *chifir*, narcotically strong tea, for the team before they went back into the zone. Pomogalov gave permission and sat down with them when they started lighting a little fire with the splinters of wood that were lying around everywhere. Matiushin sat about five steps from the fire, amazed at how familiarly the sergeant-major spoke and even laughed with the convicts, and they soon got high when they started passing the sooty tin can round the circle.

Serving in a camp had an enticing freedom to it. Life there was solitary and calm. After he started standing guard on a tower, Matiushin had unexpectedly grown unaccustomed to people, because the men were on guard duty for twenty-four hours and slept like wolves, each on his own, and came back to a barracks that was already empty, where even against their will they lived like wolves again – sleeping for the night, eating, sleeping again, and then going away again, leaving this lair to the others, whom they had seen for only ten minutes in the little guardhouse yard, during the changing of the guard, when they handed over the zone's protection. Everyone kept secrets from everyone else, everyone skulked and hid. Those who had stood their watch kept their mouths tight shut and clammed up at the slightest thing. These secrets made the guardhouse seem dark and impenetrable, but the darkness in its blank, windowless rooms was permanent in any case.

Matiushin was now familiar with the entire area around the camp, but the camp itself was quite impossible to take in at a glance. From the tower all he saw was the wasteland of the perimeter security zone and the wall of the tiny factory, the work zone. A dump of scrap metal from the little factory had been set up on waste ground very close to the security zone. Some time ago he had spotted from his tower an abandoned iron barrel that always stood in exactly the same place; at night he imagined that someone was hiding inside it. During his shift two convicts were wandering about beside the barrel when suddenly a flame erupted from it and black smoke came billowing out. That was what brought Matiushin to his senses – the sight of the smoke and the fire, and the convicts standing by the barrel. They stood there watching while the barrel smoked. Matiushin picked up the incredibly heavy receiver of the guard-post phone and reported everything to the guardhouse. After a while a warden in uniform ran out of the open gates of the production area. He dashed over to the convicts and Matiushin saw him start talking to them. But suddenly his arm straightened out abruptly at the elbow and the convict he had hit tumbled to the ground. The warder started walking round him and battering him with his boots. The other convict kept out of things and watched all this indifferently. When the warder left, the beaten convict got up. He stood still for a while, and Matiushin fancied that as the convict stood there he was looking from the distance at Matiushin, the man who had seen all this from his tower. Then the convict started shuffling about, lazily scraping sand together at his feet, walking over to the barrel and throwing it in a handful at a time. Putting the flame out. When he had extinguished it, he trudged off into the production area and didn't come back again.

In the early days of August the company's pay came in. It was issued in the orderly room, and the platoon went on guard duty in the zone, carrying their pay with them as dead weight. They persuaded Pomogalov at least to let one man go to the village shop to buy sweets, and some cigarettes too, otherwise they would have to wait another twenty-four hours. Matiushin was dying for a smoke as soon as possible, so he volunteered to be the errand boy.

It was only two hundred metres from the zone to the shop, he only had to cross the road. Stepping inside the shop, he immediately caught the smell of sausage, but at the sight of it, languishing on the counter, he stopped dead in surprise. The people in the queue were instantly filled with sudden sympathy for the soldier and started letting him push through so he could choose what he wanted. The serving woman waited hospitably. He held out the group's money and told her he wanted a kilo of sweets and some cigarettes, but he kept looking at the sausage, he couldn't tear his eyes away from it, with its glossy, greasy, natural beauty. In that moment he allowed himself to think that he could take at least a little piece. The serving woman gave him what he asked for and waited to see what else he would say; she saw him staring at the sausage. The people started egging him on.

'It's good, soldier boy, good sausage, from Tselinograd!'

And the serving woman advised him:

'Go on, take some, love, enjoy it!'

Now he couldn't leave without the sausage. For some reason he felt ashamed to seem petty in front of the people; he got completely carried away and asked for a kilogram. But while the serving woman was weighing it, he saw white bread and milk and, together with the sausage, they gave him such a deep, peaceful feeling that he shelled out for them without even a second thought.

Matiushin walked out of the shop in a hungry dream, loaded up with food, but despaired when he realised that

Oleg Pavlov

he had to take the sausage back with him to the guardhouse, from where he had been sent on his run to the
shop. He glanced around and started walking stealthily
through the village, searching with his eyes for a spot
where he could hide for a moment, but he walked right
through to the end and found himself among the veg-
etable plots, already in the steppe. Then he saw a little
trench or crater in the ground and hid on the dry earth
at the bottom of it, already anxious, as if he was being
chased. After the first few minutes, the most gluttonous,
he gagged as he was gulping down bread. He didn't finish
the bread, abandoning it in the pit, but he poured the
milk down his throat anyway, then climbed out and set
off, staggering, afraid of what he'd done, to wander back
through the dead village to the guardhouse, clutching the
group's bag of sweets and feeling sick. He couldn't see his
own bluish-grey, poisoned face, but in the guardhouse,
where they were already wondering where he'd got to,
Pomogalov started fussing over him, so Matiushin lied and
said he had started feeling unwell at the shop. But then
Pomogalov latched on to this and took it into his head to
cure him with potassium permanganate, diluting some
in a whole carafe of water and telling him:

'There's no better cure, and puking's good for you
anyway, it revitalises the organism. They say yogis live to
be a hundred years old, and why? They eat a little speck
of something and then politely squeeze it back out of
themselves, like pussycats. This permanganate brings

instant relief. Well, you blockhead, what are you gawping at? Drink it, I tell you.'

Matiushin poured a glass of it down his throat, but Pomogalov was only surprised and offended at that. He said Matiushin should drink more, half a carafe. The Chinese was hanging around in the watch officer's room, waiting to take something to the company headquarters, and the sergeant-major roped him in to take the sick man to the privy.

'Two fingers down your throat and start fighting for your life!' Pomogalov shouted cheerfully. 'Watch out he doesn't drop his head in there!'

The Chinese helped Matiushin patiently, propping him up with his shoulder and not letting him fall. Although he didn't want to get soiled, he overcame his reluctance and stayed to help to the end. However, he was startled and froze when the sick man threw up the white bread and sausage that he had gulped down. When he was done retching, Matiushin lifted up his soaking-wet face and sighed; the Chinese was standing silently one step away from him, just waiting to lead him out. But Matiushin was prepared to die rather than go back out again, realising from the severe way the titchy sergeant was looking at him that he had signed his own death sentence as far as all the soldiers were concerned. He twitched and burped up milky mush, like a little baby, but then grunted dully and reached into his pocket, pulling all the money out of it in his fist and opening his trembling hand with the dirty copper kopecks in it, so that the Chinese could see. The sergeant, realising what Matiushin was doing, silently took the money and counted it, but surprisingly enough, he seemed satisfied and tipped it into his pocket. He stood there, watching with fresh surprise and suddenly gave Matiushin a painful pinch before he felt able to leave.

Left alone in the latrine room, Matiushin dragged himself over to the sink, stuck his head under the icy water that snorted out of the nostril of the tap and gradually started coming back to life. He got a wash, slicked his hair back and set off, feeling slightly timid, to the guard room. Pomogalov was pleased with his fresh appearance and carried on doggedly singing the praises of potassium permanganate. Nothing in the guardhouse had changed in the meantime.

At night, when there was no one else awake in the guardhouse, Matiushin got hold of a pencil and a scrap of paper and scribbled a note to Yelsk. The scrap was big enough for him to report that he was alive and well and to beg to be sent ten roubles that he needed urgently in order to survive. The tears trembled in his eyes at the thought that his father and mother would hold this scrap of paper in their hands. It was as if his mother's calloused hands were holding the paper, not his own, and he simply couldn't make himself let go. The days were transformed into waiting. A letter arrived from home. The envelope was glued tightly shut, so he had to tear it patiently, but there wasn't even a single rouble inside it. Only a sheet of paper covered with his mother's lopsided, skimpy handwriting. And in everything that Alexandra Yakovlevna wrote to her son there wasn't a single word about the money that he had asked to be sent so urgently. His mother told him what she had done since that morning, as if it was all she had in her head; she wrote that she and his father were glad that he was alive and well; that in the army at least he should stop damaging his heath by smoking; and at the end there was this: 'Write to us, Vasenka. We wish you health, happiness and success in your work and studies.'

At night in the guardhouse, lying on his bunk surrounded by sleeping soldiers, Matiushin wept desolately, as if in the darkness he could see his father's miserly face and hear the cajoling, greedy voice his father had acquired after Yakov's death. You can't spare me ten roubles, but you didn't mind losing your children, damn you and curse you! After he had cursed his father, he felt calmer, his eyes closed of their own accord and he fell asleep, and then, in the middle of the night, he was shaken awake to go up on the tower.

It was a clear night. The lights of the zone, like fireflies, and the bright stars scattered across the sky were as clearly visible as two close banks of a river, and the night air flowed between them in a living, deep current, forming a bright pool in the boundless steppe. In his heart Matiushin wandered desolately along that river until dawn.

No longer grief-stricken, he drifted into the great, hazy dollops of mist. This early morning mist had an intoxicating scent of tobacco or, more likely, of the steppe and its grasses. Matiushin had been pining without anything to smoke for several days now; in the company cadging smokes or scouring around for fag ends was only for the abject losers, who always had every last kopeck of their pay taken away from them and were forced to lackey for handouts – Rebrov was already lackeying like that in the barracks and the guardhouse. Matiushin breathed the mist greedily, but there was no way he could imagine getting hold of any cigarettes. When it grew light the first local train, the very earliest, howled to announce the start of the station's day. A man set off, walking along the road from the village. After the night Matiushin was glad to see this man from his tower, but suddenly he noticed that the man was puffing out smoke; he was walking along and smoking. Just then the man drew level with the tower and in his solitude he looked up at the soldier who happened to be close by and waved his hand in greeting. If he hadn't waved, Matiushin wouldn't have done what then simply happened of its own accord, one word following another, when he called the man and the man stopped guiltily in the road.

'Got any smokes? Let me have one, do me a favour!'

'How can I?' said the little man, turning his face up, but he was willing to do the favour and hovered beside the fence.

The Matiushin Case

The little man was standing so close that Matiushin didn't have the strength to let him go, and the man wanted to help anyway; Matiushin called to him.

'Come a bit closer at least, there's a gap just down there.'

The nearest towers were about two hundred metres away. Figuring out warily how to avoid being spotted, Matiushin convinced himself that no one would see anything. The little man had a very simple appearance, like a worker – probably a railway linesman, and no officer or screw could be walking to the station at this time. It only needed a minute. Matiushin flew down onto the path. The little man, himself anxious, fearfully thrust a cigarette through the gap, and since Matiushin didn't have any matches of his own, he hastily lit up from the man's lighted stub. Then they flew apart, an identical sense of relief in their hearts.

Matiushin's blissful, light feeling as he puffed on the cigarette clutched in his fist, fresh and hot, and watched the little man disappearing into the distance along the weightless morning road, didn't last for long: he heard a vague noise from the direction of the guardhouse and soon a squad of soldiers, running at top speed, was cast up onto the path as if from the bottom of the sea. First he saw a radio and the crescent shape of an antenna behind one soldier's back, then he saw Pomogalov's peaked cap and turned cold, thinking that there was an attack or a breakout somewhere on the perimeter of the camp.

The squad rolled up to his tower in a rumbling wave and surrounded it without a word. They didn't run any further, but looked up at him in anger and surprise from the path. Pomogalov straightened his cap and started climbing up unhurriedly. He shouted threateningly to Matiushin to unlock the little door, as if Matiushin wasn't standing guard on a tower, but had locked himself in somewhere and was trying to hold them off.

Pomogalov waved his nose about in the tense silence and calmed down.

'Right, you bastard, had a good smoke? Do you know what you get for a cigarette break like that? And where did you go for the cigarette – into the zone, was it? What were you smoking? Are you fooling around with grass? I get it . . . we're playing dumb.'

Without another word, the sergeant-major climbed heavily down the tower and the squad marched back to the guardhouse. Matiushin finished his watch. Dybenko arrived in the morning with the new guard, and although no one else said anything, he laughed.

'Well now, suicide boy, they say you got hold of some smokes from the zone? Did the cons pay you a visit and give you a puff? Well, well! Did you tempt them by offering them vodka, or did they tempt you? And why did you kick up such a ruckus, you fool? I told you: it's too soon for you yet, keep your nose out!'

Matiushin couldn't help smiling himself at that as he looked at the silent and oddly bitter faces around him, guardhouse: he knew all about everything and had come to hold an investigation, but when he heard from the sergeant-major that Matiushin was scouring the latrine, he disdainfully decided not to meet him and was even piqued about something. No full investigation took place. Matiushin was called by the dejected sergeant-major, who passed on the political officer's instructions to leave the guardhouse and his post and walk to company head-quarters unarmed. When he arrived in the barracks, think-ing he was going to an interrogation, Arman's new order was waiting for him, transmitted in equally disdainful fashion via the day orderly: take a rag and a basin and wash the floors in all the rooms. The company barracks was a two-storey building and this job had never been done by one man because he would have been crawling around on the floors all night long. Realising that this was a continuation of his punishment, Matiushin took off his tunic in order not to get it dirty and set to work, running out to the summer washing area to change the water in the battered aluminium basin. As he was running like this he met Karpovich, whom he hadn't seen anywhere for a long time except for the changeovers at the guardhouse, when one platoon handed over to the other. Karpovich stopped, clearly not in any hurry, and looked at him sadly.

'I've heard how things are with you: you caused a real uproar in the zone. So they've decided you won't go out on guard duty any longer. Arman wants to make you the permanent cleaner, so think on that, my cunning lad.'

Matiushin turned away and strode off to finish washing the barracks, feeling his back shuddering as the other man watched him go. That evening at the roll call Arman ordered Matiushin to step forward out of the line and announced to the first platoon that Matiushin would no longer be going out on guard duty. And then the next day, after ordering Matiushin to step forward out of the line again, he announced to the second platoon that he was appointing Matiushin as the cleaner.

On Sunday Matiushin was taken to the military prosecutor's office instead of the bathhouse. The sergeant-major rode in the prison truck with him again, but he was taciturn and angry.

The old two-storey mansion of the military prosecutor's office looked like a henhouse, and even in summer it seemed chilly and rotten, so Matiushin trod cautiously on the squeaking floorboards, afraid that they would fall apart, and he stared in amazement at the doors beside which sickly-looking soldiers were sitting, waiting to be seen, like at a doctor's. The duty investigator turned out to be a youthful lieutenant, thin, with a pointy-nosed face. Overjoyed that a son had been born to him the night before, he spoke rather soulfully with Pomogalov and peered wearily with his sleepless eyes at the document sent with Matiushin, trying to make sense of it as he reluctantly started the interrogation. However, in the course of that interrogation Matiushin discovered the most important thing for him: that morning a signalling device on the door of his tower had been tripped and it had sent the alarm to the guardhouse.

It was pointless trying to deny it, so he confessed to having left his post, but he gave the same answer to all the questions after that: he went down the tower to relieve himself. Pomogalov barked at him, ashamed, and jumped up off his chair, all set to leave, because he suddenly couldn't bear the investigation any longer. The lieutenant took pity on him and flushed, nodding provocatively in Matiushin's direction.

'Well go out for an hour or so if you like, dad, get some fresh air, we'll soon beat out of him what he needed to relieve himself of, we'll stick him behind bars.'

'Ah, that's clear enough, he just needed a pee. He's not stupid . . . They don't court-martial you for that . . . ' Pomogalov exclaimed in exasperation. 'You won't beat anything out of him. Look at him, you couldn't beat a speck of dust out of someone like that. It's just Arman playing the fool – he's the one who needs to be taught a lesson, he needs his face smashed against the desk. You know, they were all officers in his family, oh yes, and he boasts about his French blood. You know, they ended up with us when that Napoleon came over here. So they're fucking Napoleons. And the prick's a noble too, of course! Just give him some men so that he can lean hard on them, he'll enjoy that, show everyone what he's made of, he'll be a big man, maybe a marshal, a triple Hero of the Soviet Union. He hasn't got a life of his own and he won't let

The sergeant was called Dojo. He kept company with the trainer of the army dogs. There was a little world apart, an enclosure with a wire fence the height of a man, out on the edge of the company's territory, where they kept the Alsatians in cages in the summer and in an outbuilding during the winter cold season. Matiushin wasn't supposed to clear up after the Alsatians but, one day, Dojo lay in wait for him at a deserted spot and started pinching him fiercely and hissing that from now on he should go to clean out the dogs' enclosure and do what the trainer told him.

With time Matiushin started recognising the Alsatians and telling their personalities apart. A black male with the nickname German, the trainer's favourite, took a dislike to him. There were also two stupid young bitches who barked at Matiushin as soon he approached the cages and, although they were in sections at opposite ends of the enclosure, they flung themselves at the wire at the same moment, barked together and calmed down together. The best dog was an old bitch who had worked in the army for some time. When he walked into her cage she lay there calmly with her head between her paws, looked at the broom and realised that he had come to clean up. Later Matiushin started smelling so strongly of the dogs' shit that she probably didn't even think of him as a man any more but a working dog like them who walked on two paws. In her cage Matiushin could always take a rest and have a smoke – the old Alsatian gladly shared that time with him. She kept an eye on every movement he made, and if something started slipping out of her field of view, she turned her head or changed her lying position so that she could see everything. That was the way she kept her own order.

Cleaning out the cages was no longer an oppressive burden for Matiushin. He realised that he was doing something for the Alsatians that they couldn't do for themselves, like children. The trainer sensed this and tried to think up even filthier work, but at the same time he started trusting Matiushin more. He was jealous: he didn't let the soldiers near the Alsatians and the Alsatians didn't like the men very much, but seeing that Matiushin had come to love the Alsatians and was making an effort, the trainer trusted him to feed and walk them. Matiushin hid himself away there. The only person who visited him was Karpovich. That is, it looked as if he came to visit Matiushin but what really took him to the dogs' enclosure was some kind of business with the trainer and the Chinese, who called him into the outbuilding, from which they would all emerge about five minutes later, one at a time, glancing around; Karpovich would come out looking either furtive and resentful or smiling and contented. After emerging hurriedly from the outbuilding, he never simply went his own way, but sat down beside Matiushin and started up long conversations that lasted a lot longer than those five minutes. He either complained or boasted, calling everyone bastards, trusting Matiushin with all his hopes and dreams, but the moment he was asked about those strange meetings in the outbuilding he either fell silent or tried to turn it into a joke.

Karpovich himself remained a mystery to Matiushin. One day he said he was tired and wanted to clear out and that he had a plan for doing it. One man in the company who hated him was Dybenko. But it turned out that this was to Karpovich's advantage, and he even deliberately tried to rile Dybenko. That way, when Karpovich wanted, he would easily be able to make Dybenko furious, and all he needed was for someone to give him a really hard beating. Then he would end up in the hospital and, after that, it was all very simple: he would go home, because of his injuries, and Dybenko, who had injured him, would be condemned to a disciplinary battalion – and all legal and above board!

Matiushin believed Karpovich, although it was sickening to know and understand what he was keeping up his sleeve. From that day on Matiushin kept that secret as if it was his own, as if he too could break out and be free. The repair work crept over from the zone to the barracks, so that the men entered it along ramps, straight through the window into the sleeping area, which was partitioned off with scaffolding, with the beds shifted into one corner. Prisoners on work release were brought in to do the painting and whitewashing: they wandered around the barracks, pestering the soldiers for matches or cigarettes. For lack of space the soldiers slept two men to a bed. On 1st September Arman went away on leave, disappearing from the company just as cleanliness, peace and order had disappeared from it.

By the time that man left, all the floor-washing amid the dirt of the repairs, the clambering in through windows and sleeping in heaps, had left Matiushin without any feelings, thoughts or desires, and every day he merely waited drearily for something that was hovering in the air, which had been made new and strange by the smell of fresh paint drying. Then Karpovich started to irritate him with his meaningless conversations: Matiushin would probably have beaten Karpovich himself, and he even imagined it more than once when his reason or patience was exhausted. Karpovich's complaining and groaning roused an incomprehensible fury in him. They seemed to come from some other life, they were alien and unnecessary, just a heap of petty junk.

But one day there was loud shouting and everybody ran to the mess, where it sounded as if someone was being killed. Karpovich was lying on the floor, screaming terribly, his face bloodied and his eyes staring wildly, while the cook Gadjiev towered over him. At the slightest sign of movement he beat Karpovich about the head and arms with a ladle. The men simply surrounded the site of this bloodletting but no one interfered, and in any case Gadjiev wasn't the kind of man who could be subdued even by a crowd like that. He had ended up as a cook during his first year in the army, after shooting a runaway from his tower.

He was given home leave and, when he came back, he was transferred to work in the mess. That was the unwritten rule because if he had stayed on his tower, he might never have served out his time: the convicts would have done for him in revenge. Gadjiev was in clover as a cook, he had power in the company, but he was afraid of the zone and rarely left the cook's quarters except at night, for a breath of air. Matiushin stood in the crowd with everyone else, astonished that Karpovich's plan was being realised, although he saw the cook there, instead of Dybenko. But the Chinese came running up and the crowd slunk away. Nothing was said about taking Karpovich to the hospital. The titchy sergeant led the platoon off to the zone, as usual, and Karpovich, who had already washed himself down and seemed pleased about something, marched off to go on duty with the rest of them.

Twenty-four hours passed. The platoon came back and, in the arms room, while they were handing in their guns and the bullets from their automatic clips, and the duty officer was signing for them, Karpovich suddenly started rushing about and howling, even weeping: after twenty-four hours on guard duty his clip was three live bullets short. When the duty officer realised that Karpovich wasn't playing the fool and all this wasn't just a joke, he ordered Karpovich to be held there while he ran off to get his superior. Karpovich was led away and interrogated all night long, and in the dormitory, which was on the same floor, they could hear him weeping and groaning. Whispers ran round the beds in the dark. Everybody understood what had happened. Matiushin understood too. In the guardhouse after every watch you handed in your rifle to the arms locker, but the pouch with the automatic clip had to stay with you throughout the twenty-four hours of guard duty, so you walked and ate and slept with it on your belt, ready for action the moment the signal came. If even a single bullet disappeared, a court martial was inevitable, and then the disciplinary battalion, even though the only proof of guilt was the fact that the bullet had disappeared. But that was exactly why Karpovich couldn't have robbed himself, just as he couldn't have lost those bullets, jammed into the automatic clip. Someone had opened his pouch, probably when he was sleeping, taken out the clip, clicked out those three bullets and then put the clip back into the pouch without Karpovich feeling anything or noticing when he went to his tower afterwards. One of their own must have done it, someone who had walked along the path with him to the same watch – or Dojo; someone who could have been in the guardhouse dormitory at the same time as he was and pretended to be sleeping.

The air was tense with fear, as if those bullets were about to go off. The fear ebbed away the next day when Karpovich was taken to the special section at regimental headquarters and didn't come back to the company. Matiushin caught a glimpse of him being led out of the barracks; he was walking rapidly, seeming withdrawn, staring at the ground as if he were butting the officer walking in front of him with his head.

At the Alsatians' enclosure the emptiness left after Karpovich's departure was filled by a strange kind of depression. This was the place that he had visited most often. Something was languishing here, as if Karpovich's soul was lurking, prowling about in secret. The trainer kept glancing at Matiushin with a probing, otherworldly expression, as if he was suspicious and wary of something. He didn't go over to the outbuilding any longer, and for some reason Dojo didn't visit him either. Pomogalov sometimes came over furtively to the dogs' enclosure and every time after one of his visits the trainer was sullen and angry and completely out of sorts. He let the Alsatians out to run free and shut himself away in the outbuilding for long periods. When the Chinese and the trainer invited Matiushin into it he was surprised to see what it was like inside: heaped up with old, worn-out clothes, flasks and cooking pots, transformed into a storage room, where the only empty spaces were the kennels in the corners. The trainer suddenly held out a flask to him.

'Take a swallow, we've got plenty of this stuff.'

Matiushin took a sip from the flask, and when he felt the strange drink scorch his throat, he realised indifferently that it wasn't vodka and it wasn't wine, but some kind of home-brewed moonshine. The Chinese smiled, pleased.

The next day Matiushin was assigned to guard duty in the zone. He remembered those new days – clear but colourless. The company's pig died: it had eaten some barbed wire on the dump when the swineherd wasn't watching. Gadjiev boiled up the dead animal's flesh into a thick meat jelly that looked like ham, and they stuffed themselves with it in the guardhouse. In the middle of the day Matiushin went out to take a break from the food; the guardhouse yard had got too cramped and the soldiers who weren't up on their towers crept outside, onto the road. There were several women of indeterminate age, who had probably come to meet husbands in the camp, hovering about at the camp reception point, various people from the village were strolling past along the road, and a bus was waiting at the gates: a body was brought out to it on a stretcher from the zone, and then another one. The convicts lay there quietly. They were alive, but one of them, a young guy, had a hunk of metal sticking out of his chest and he was holding it with his hands. When the warders started loading up the stretchers, the young guy got frightened and started groaning. The stretchers were put in the passage between the seats, so when the bus drove away from the zone it looked empty.

The night was over. The tower on which Matiushin had spent it was always called the 'vodka tower' by the locals – in the guardhouse and the zone and the village – but he had only understood why this night, although everyone else seemed to know. The sergeant-major had frisked the squad before they went out onto the path, but now Matiushin realised that these searches were always meaningless. He left the guardhouse empty-handed. During the night shift, flasks full of moonshine were brought to the tower by the Chinese and the trainer, who completed an inspection tour round the path at least every hour. The booze had already been ordered by the zone, so this night they were delivering to the zone what they had taken money for in advance. After guard duty Matiushin was supposed to receive his share from the trainer in the outbuilding. The trainer and the Chinese didn't tell him who had taken the orders from the convicts on the other side of the barbed wire or where the moonshine came from. He had to do his own job: take the risk of receiving the flasks at the tower and tossing them into the zone to the messengers who named the right name and, at the same time, if necessary, accepting new orders.

After the change of guard at the end of those twenty-four hours, Pomogalov didn't release him with the platoon – he ordered him to hand in his rifle to Dojo and said he should follow him. They dropped back from the others and went through a little door in the camp gates, coming out into a blank dead end that looked like a yard, beside a different set of gates. Here at the guardhouse lodge, a delivery from the zone had been left for the sergeant-major: weighty rolls of polythene, the height of a man. Pomogalov slung one onto his own shoulder and Matiushin shouldered the other and set off in step with the sergeant-major. Anybody wandering along unburdened who met them on the way greeted Pomogalov respectfully as they approached and he replied:

'And good health to you too!'

They walked as far as a brick house surrounded by a high fence. The sergeant-major pushed open the wicket in the iron gates, which were as ugly to look at as the camp gates, but inside them was a quiet, well-kept yard with chickens, where Pomogalov was met by his daughter, who was playing with her father's shoes on the porch, an intelligent-looking Alsatian that made no sound but watched Matiushin keenly, and a round, sturdy woman who came hurrying out at the noise. They dumped the rolls beside the skeleton of a fresh new greenhouse and Pomogalov strode over to the lavatory with a sigh. The moment he walked into the yard, his daughter had attached herself to him and started following him about, and she didn't notice the soldier who had come with him. The young wife went into the house and came out with a piece of pie, but Pomogalov rebuked her sternly.

'Why not pour him a glass of vodka as well, you fool! Come on now, no spoiling my soldiers. That's how it is, lad. You haven't deserved my pies yet.'

After the sergeant-major had dumped his load, he straightened up and squared his shoulders. In his own home he seemed like a colder and greedier man than when he was striding about with a tired, understanding expression on duty, where he didn't begrudge anything.

'I'm not blind,' sighed Pomogalov. 'I see that you've sneaked back onto guard duty. Ok, so stand duty while our little Frenchman is bathing in the sea. It's not my headache. Go for it, rake it in. But if anything happens, son, I'll have your hide and hang it out to dry. You need the nose of a wolf round here. You know what did for Karpovich? He kept his money with Gadjiev, thought it would be as good as in the savings bank in those pots and pans of his. But when Karpovich wanted all his savings back, the cook gave the nod – and that was the end of Karpovich. And look at how it was done: neat and tidy, all legal and above board! Well, why are you cringing like that? Ok, drop it, I'm not the little Frenchman, and this isn't the prosecutor's office, but I know you earned yourself a tenner last night. Everybody knows that, son, that's just the way things are. So just you think, think on . . . Now, all right! Svetlanka, pour me and the soldier boy a big one each!'

With an incredulous air, the woman brought out a clean, domestic-looking bottle from somewhere.

'My own stuff!' said the sergeant-major, nodding in satisfaction at the bottle, and added rather strangely: 'Remember . . . Remember Karpovich, son!'

They flogged the booze into the zone in flasks and even in hot water bottles, as if they were deliberately running down their stocks, dumping it. They were in a hurry. They took risks. Matiushin fearlessly ordered himself a new pair of tarpaulin boots in the zone and replaced his old, darned ones that every dog in the regiment knew. His new boots didn't have just a whiff of the zone about them, they reeked of it. The deputy commander for political affairs came back from leave, bringing fine rain and cold weather to go with his mood, although he himself had got a tan and looked fitter. He made enquiries and saw what had happened in the company but didn't say anything, and Matiushin carried on standing guard duty – on the vodka tower.

The Chinese and the trainer were a bit dejected and trade quietened down, but only for a while, and there was no way Matiushin could get away from the vodka tower. Even the money – the reason he was handling the booze – started to frighten him. Sometimes in the guardhouse he was overcome by fear that they would hold a search, and only calmed down after he had dropped the money beyond reach in the privy.

A month later, in October, they heard about Karpovich. A company convoy escorted convicts to the pre-trial detention centre in Karaganda, and while they were there they got talking with the prison guards, who boasted that they had a soldier with red shoulder tabs awaiting trial there and his cellmates had already made him their bitch; his name was Karpovich. When they got back from the convoy, the company men couldn't wait to shock everyone with the news; they went round the barracks as if they were dragging a dead cat by its tail. The rumour even reached the zone via the 'convoy post'. The convicts yelled mockingly to the tower men from the roofs of their barracks huts, saying they should send Karpovich to them under escort. But the soldiers set out into the zone to take revenge. At night, in the guardhouse, volunteers were gathered to take a stroll to the punishment cells where the non-cooperating prisoners and criminal bosses were held: Dybenko went round the prisoners one by one and afterwards he told everyone how he and the others went into a cell, announced that they were taking revenge on the organised criminals on behalf of a soldier, handcuffed the prisoners and beat seven shades of shit out of them.

That was when Matiushin decided that he would just grab about three hundred roubles and run. If he screwed the price up, there wouldn't be a peep out of the convicts – dealing in booze had got more risky. He felt his own strength in the fact that he had a goal – to escape. Escape. Stick the money in his boot – and bolt into the hospital. If he couldn't manage it by cunning, he'd have to smash his head open against the wall or pay off the doctors. The hospital was the most important thing, he needed them to send him to be checked for something really serious, so he could be declared unfit, an invalid. Escape, escape! And if everything was coming together as Matiushin suspected, he needed to get into that hospital quick, or the November winds would start howling and the frosty winter would set in, harder than death. He sensed the approach of winter very keenly.

However, in the same way as they could sometimes tell in a camp when someone was planning an escape, Arman seemed to sense that Matiushin had made up his mind and was almost ready to run. The searches and checks became more frequent, with the political officer suddenly appearing in the guardhouse in the middle of the night. And he virtually chained Matiushin to it, putting him on guardhouse duty – demobilised men had been leaving one by one and no new soldiers had arrived in the regiment yet, so they all had to serve for two men, but Matiushin was the only one the political officer kept in the guardhouse day after day without a change of watch.

Matiushin lived in the guardhouse and never went off duty but, more than that, instead of the sleep he was entitled to, Arman sent him to work on the reinforcements. Mountains of sand had been brought to the four sides of the zone and they were spreading it along chains of men with spades, then scattering it and levelling it out with harrows. The harrows were made especially for the men: a pipe was welded in an arc, like a tow bar, to a serrated iron pile. Three men at a time got into a harrow, leaned their chests against the pipe and dragged it until the sand had been dispersed. And then they went back, flung the harrow onto the mounds that other soldiers had heaped up with their spades and dragged it forward, covering the exclusion zone with an even layer of sand. After dragging a harrow about, Matiushin marched off to the vodka tower, and after that he got into harness again,

someone to be there. His eyes watered with bright tears and he spoke without a pause, not even looking at Matiushin, squinting blindly, his gaze aimed somewhere to one side. Matiushin didn't have the strength to leave. He didn't even stir from the spot, dissolving in the man's voice as if into oblivion, with a sweet kind of pain. Sagging over their heads with the paint flaking off it, the tiny room's low, oppressive plywood ceiling didn't seem like a ceiling at all but a gaping breach, a hole. Even the prison corridor, which was the only entrance to the zone via the building and was protected by the ugly barred window of this little room squeezed into two square metres, seemed like a breach and a hole, with its armoured doors, locks and bolts and its fur coat of cold, naked concrete instead of walls.

The automatic dangling from Matiushin's shoulder, which he hadn't handed in to the arms locker, looked as dead-beat and exhausted as Matiushin really was, although he seemed as tough as iron. Even though the bustle and confusion had settled down long ago and the watch rooms were deathly quiet with sleeping men, Matiushin carried on wasting away his rest time with this little soldier who was condemned not to sleep, penned in between these four walls, knowing that he himself would never get enough sleep, and also feeling penned in, his bones squeezed tight into a little room where it was easier to stand than sit – and easier to die than live.

He refused to believe that this time of his had been counted and there would be no way for him to grab even a short minute of sleep when they drove him back out to the tower. It also pained him that those men who were sleeping like babies on the other side of the wall didn't have the strength simply to swallow down their own hunger and weakness and not prolong them sickeningly, day after day, but he also hated them because, although he was among them, he was different, alien, as if he was some freak who wouldn't be able to hold out for long on his own. That is, he hated them as if he knew that he was inexorably fated to be killed because of them, among them, but his very blood ached compassionately with a live-born, brutal love that might flare up in a furious impulse and make him shoot every one of the sleepers so that they wouldn't be tormented day after day, so that these innocent babes wouldn't be forced, day after day, day after day, to live.

Feeling painfully unnecessary even to himself, Matiushin suddenly became aware what a secure human position he held in this little room, as if he, not the controller, were in charge here. He also realised that the ginger guy needed him, couldn't manage without him, although there was nothing in the company to make them friends, and Matiushin even resented this hardy controller's easy desk duties – although that too, surprisingly, bonded them together, setting each of them precisely in his place. Matiushin forgave the ginger guy for his ignoble desk job, realising that his own guard duty on the tower had earned him a stronger position than the controller in this quiet little room of his, where he even paid for attention with sweets . . .

Matiushin awoke from his stupor – he fancied that he had heard a scream far away in the night. He was instantly flooded with strength, intent on the silence, but he couldn't hear anything – and then, literally a moment later, there was a lingering clamour, a howling and screaming from the direction of the zone that rolled on and on, growing like a snowball: someone was running towards the checkpoint, yelling at the top of his lungs. In that instant the ginger guy froze, surprised and fearful, looking helplessly to Matiushin, then took fright at the automatic rifle on which Matiushin had already jerked the breech lock, readying himself, and was now waiting.

'Don't shoot, don't shoot!'

'Shut up, you fool!' Matiushin hissed, not knowing what was going to happen to them. 'I . . . '

A screaming warder came dashing into the checkpoint area like a wild boar and rushed desperately towards the first set of bars blocking the corridor, which couldn't be unlocked from the outside, because the bolt mechanism of the barred gate was controlled from the little room, from the checkpoint.

The warder was unharmed except for a split eyebrow, but a little lake of blood had flooded his eye, and he was goggling wildly with the crimson bubble, unable to see anything through the caked blood. Not knowing that it was only his eyebrow that was split, the warder was shuddering and trembling as if his eye had been gouged out. He screeched sickeningly, squealing that there was a bloody massacre in the barracks and pressing himself against the bars in terror as if someone was pursuing him, hot on his heels, to gouge out his remaining eye and kill him; he was sobbing in his desperation to break into the shelter of the guardhouse. The iron frame of the barred door shook under his assault, seeming suddenly no heavier than a cobweb although he was only scrabbling on the spot, twitching convulsively as he dangled there in its net.

The ginger guy started staggering towards the door but he didn't have the heart to run, and he looked tear-fully back at Matiushin, afraid to unlock the barred door himself and let the wounded, squealing warder into the guardhouse. The warder, realising that the soldiers could leave him there, that their orders were the most important thing for them, started cursing them with implacable spite, demanding that they obey him, like a berserk woman.

'Don't let him in: that might be just what they're waiting for!' Matiushin said firmly, and the warder gave a bloodcurdling howl:

'I hate you, you bas-ta-a-ards . . . ' The buttons of his uniform clattered as they slithered down over the bars and his carcass slumped onto the grey concrete floor.

Matiushin thought it was hilarious, everything sud-denly seemed funny to him; the more hopelessly dark and confused it became, the funnier it was, but he too was alternately shuddering with cold and suffocating in the heat. He dashed out into the guard room and started yelling. The ginger guy rushed to Arman's watch officer's room – and then it began.

Many of them didn't have their boots on yet and were dragging them along behind, some had given up looking for their boots and were jostling fearfully, barefoot, around the arms locker. Some who had automatics were staggering from one corner to another without any orders, without anyone in command. But suddenly the real alarm signal was howling, and then the soldiers started thrashing about in a frenzy, thrusting each other aside, trampling over each other. Whose idea was it to turn on the siren? The soldiers were up and the siren only disorientated them, it was so deafening. Matiushin was overwhelmed by the siren's howling too, but he went dashing blindly into the formation, and although he didn't know the authorised sequence of personnel, something led him to occupy the right place, or perhaps it wasn't his, but anyway he was there with everyone.

They set off at a rush, hurtling forward with the Alsatians dashing along in a pack at the front. The dogs were swept along by a kind of frenzy that wasn't in the men, but the soldiers ran just as furiously, spurred on by the howling of the siren. The only reason Matiushin knew he was still alive was this being pressed up against the others, being at one with them. With so many men around you, it's not possible to believe in death. Or perhaps it was the hope somewhere inside him that his death would fall on another man: the one who was panting hard at Matiushin's back, or the one whose head was right there in front of Matiushin. The strongest feeling of all, though, was that nobody could be killed: that Lady Death, if she existed, would be afraid of so many men, would overshoot and miss her target. He couldn't keep up with his thoughts about death, unable to work out if he was dashing towards or running away from it, or what kind of night this was; like an animal, he was swept away by a single, headlong, mighty feeling, a clash of all the human impulses – love, hate, despair, fear – that existed separately in his soul but had suddenly united into one vital, living force, as if another heart had started beating beside his first heart, and Matiushin, who couldn't even cope with one life, suddenly had two lives in his chest.

They ran along the cramped, narrow path between the rows of wire fencing, jostling and bumping into each other. Yet for some reason Matiushin fancied that there was open space all around them. And suddenly a hand pulled him out, and someone shook him and shouted at him to stay there and not move from the spot. Matiushin realised he had been left alone. The ground skulked in the darkness under his feet. He was surrounded by a confusion of fences, crooked rows of wire, the searing, harsh, white beams of searchlights.

The Alsatians' barking carried on, but it was like dull flashes. If something was happening, it was a long way from Matiushin. The soldiers standing on the path one span of wire away from him were already smoking – he spotted the little lights. His heart kept alternately freezing and exploding, shifting about inside him. Soon a new, uncertain light appeared. Day was beginning and the searchlights began to fade, as usual. Morning came. Men close to each other in the cordon started waving their arms and calling out. It was as if they had discovered each other.

Matiushin exchanged shouts with the sentries; none of them knew what had happened in the zone that night – from the towers they couldn't see, but they had heard some kind of ruckus over by the barracks.

When morning was established, he grew weary again, with the uncertainty and the waiting. It began to drizzle. But then his squad appeared on the path. They were slouching along, angry. The men were leaving the cordon of their own accord and swarming into the guardhouse.

Matiushin wanted to sleep, especially now that this futile night had become even less comprehensible. The only thing that kept him on his feet was that he still had to march as far as the guardhouse. He was so burnt-out that he slept as he walked. His thoughts and feelings drifted along on their own and it was like waking up when he suddenly realised that he was still thinking about something, feeling something and drifting along, without even knowing what for or where to. He couldn't even grasp that all the bunks in the sleeping area had been taken long ago so there wouldn't be anywhere for him to lie down and he would have to wait. About half the platoon was left without places in the guardhouse. Those who had stood through the night in the cordon were all without bunks. Matiushin lay down on a bench in the little mess room and fell into a dead sleep. The only thing he had time to feel was a tremulous, bitter unity with all the men: that they had all burnt themselves out together, and now they were falling asleep together, and the same silence was lulling them all.

He was shaken awake at breakfast time, to free up the table – the rations had been brought from the barracks on a trolley. Matiushin dragged himself off the bench and, enveloped in a kind of mist, he chewed up a mess tin of hot mushy peas. He marched off to the tower and suffered through his shift there. Arriving back at the guardhouse like a corpse, Matiushin thought that now at last he would catch up on his sleep, all legal and above board: according to regulations he was supposed to sleep now. However the soldiers weren't allowed into the sleeping area in the guardhouse. Those who were sleeping had been driven out into the yard long before this reveille. He had the idea that the political officer wanted to exercise his power and that was why he was keeping everyone out in the yard – but where would that get him? He'd just mock them a bit and then have to let them sleep anyway. He needed to rehabilitate himself in his own eyes, but the men needed their rest too, otherwise they'd break down. If the officer couldn't let it go, it meant his petty little soul had taken a serious battering. It meant he'd screwed things up and he knew it; in his own heart he sensed that he was no hero. With this thought, that the political officer knew all this, it would be equally pleasant for Matiushin to stand sleeplessly to attention or to sleep: go on, torment yourself, little officer; eat your heart out.

A feeble, irritating rain with hardly any water in it had been falling without a break since the morning. They were lined up for Arman. Matiushin recognised his voice from the very first words. But even the pitiful, soaking-wet rank of men, this chaotic bunch, this human trash had hustled itself together in a common clumsy impulse to line up in front of him and look like men. But the political officer suddenly flared up and shouted at them, no longer seeing their eyes or faces or even, it seemed, the men themselves:

'What kind of way is that to hold your rifles? Lower the barrels! Barrels down!'

They were still standing in the yard in damp monkey jackets, as if they were up to their chests in the ground, and Matiushin was already cursing the officer and this fine rain and he wanted to get under some kind of roof as soon as possible. Delaying the change of guard for longer and longer, Arman shouted that last night they had all insulted his honour as an officer.

He's found himself someone to blame, the little officer's exonerated himself, Matiushin thought. That night the political officer had been too cowardly to go into the zone to find out what was happening. He had rushed around behind their backs, like that warder who had stuck his nose into a barracks hut in the middle of a fight and gone running off to holler about it. It wasn't clear who Arman had saved either. He'd driven the soldiers who didn't know what was going on into that barracks instead of himself, although the convicts had long ago separated their own men and even carried one wounded man to the hospital. But now the political officer had gathered his wits and was striding to and fro; he'd started tediously summing up the night: who had committed what blunders, what all the commotion was about, how the soldiers had behaved on the towers and in the cordon. Now the events had acquired a clear outline for him, a kind of glassy transparency, and he had a very coherent understanding of what had happened and when.

Finally he stated what everyone already knew – that last night a prisoner had been killed in the zone: the man had been stabbed in the zone in a drunken fight, a troublemaker, and finally given up the ghost in hospital. Drinking bouts had become more frequent in the zone. Someone in the company, someone *here* was in contact with the prisoners and was selling liquor.

It could never have occurred to Matiushin that the political officer would decide to punish everyone for the vodka tower by launching a devastating frontal attack. He started feeling sick and fury stirred inside him, but it was powerless fury, which is even more terrible. Has it begun? It has begun! This was the way it was now: it was life or death.

Matiushin suddenly realised that Arman was watching him, keeping his eyes on him. And Matiushin froze: so that was Arman's plan, he was roasting Matiushin like this, and he kept turning up the heat, directing it straight at him. Matiushin tried not to tremble so the men would see how staunchly he was holding out. He fancied that the soldiers would outlast Arman: they'd been standing for an hour already, but no one had flinched yet. Arman had miscalculated here. Overstepped the mark, not even bothered to hold a secret interrogation with each of them separately. Maybe in secret and out of sight they would have informed on each other. But he wanted them to inform in front of everyone, so that it would be a kind of group denunciation – he wanted to humiliate and debase the whole platoon. Or he was expecting that Matiushin himself wouldn't be able to stand it. What Arman wanted, clearly, was not an informer but a witness – that was what he had set his sights on; he wanted proof, not hints and whispers. Arman knew, just as everyone here knew everything about everyone else, but just let him try to prove it. And he wouldn't get a witness like that out of the soldiers, not even if he buried the entire platoon in the guardhouse for ever. No one would testify.

Then, with a solemn air, Arman went off into the guardhouse, leaving the soldiers quiet and shaken by what had just taken place in the little yard. Everybody waited desolately for the political officer to come back out to the ranks, but Arman didn't appear and the yard started buzzing drearily.

Pomogalov came on duty as the watch officer and relieved the political officer, but the men weren't relieved, the entire platoon was left there and given another twenty-four hours of guard duty as punishment. Hiding away in the little room, Matiushin drank *chifir*. He wasn't going anywhere; he'd had enough. He wasn't going to budge from the spot, not even if they dragged him. He'd stood his watch and, even if they drove the platoon out onto the towers, let those whose turn it was march out: he was on leave and he was going to drink *chifir* and get warm. Hearing them assembling men into a squad as another hellish twenty-four hours began, Matiushin swore painfully in his fury, but immediately his strength faded, leaving him weak, and his burnt-out soul stopped feeling anything at all, yet he understood with his *chifir*-numbed mind that things had turned out wrong, they'd turned out even worse, and there was no way they could have turned out better. Matiushin sipped *chifir* and everything around was quiet. Everyone had accepted that they were staying on duty. Some strode into the squad, some headed for the bunks to catch up on their sleep. And Matiushin suddenly thought that it was actually good to stay for a second turn, otherwise he would have had to get up, get in line and march, and he wouldn't have been able to finish his *chifir*. His eyes were gluing themselves shut and he dozed off with the mug in his hand. For what seemed a single, brief moment everything went dim in front of his eyes and a warm, sweet mist embraced him. But he opened his eyes and the mist dispersed. They shook him awake to go to the tower. His three hours had run out. Matiushin's feet carried him along the path of their own accord, as if he was moving through water. Not over the surface but just above the very bottom, he was pulled along by a slow, deep current. And everything was good. It was warm, calm and easy, but there wasn't any air, he was filled up to his throat with flabby water, like lead.

PART FOUR

Some great brute had squashed him up on the bunk . . .
The pushy soldier was clearly one of those who had stood
on the towers from the early twilight until midnight and
got thoroughly chilled in the blustery steppe wind. They'd
come back to the guardhouse at the latest change-over and
were waiting for the commander to get the other squad
up off the well-warmed bunks so that it would be their
turn to thaw themselves out with someone else's warmth
and grab an hour or two of sleep until they were roused
again. But this one hadn't been able to wait, clearly he was
completely shattered. In the darkness Matiushin couldn't
make out his face. The soldier and he were lying with
their sides against each other and the soldier was sound
asleep, but Matiushin had been woken by the other man's
dogged determination. He didn't have the willpower to
fall asleep now, even though he was so sleepy . . . If he'd
been told to lie down on stones, he would have lain down
on stones, just as long as he knew that on those stones
no one would wake him. Just a short sleep, really deep.
Sometimes it happened that the commander woke them

to go on duty and, in the bustle of the general preparations, someone would decide to snooze for a moment, lie back down on the bunk until the others were ready and fall so deeply asleep that he had to be dragged out of the dormitory by force and then doused with water.

After the previous night Matiushin was barely alive. And he needed to get some sleep, at least now between watches. But he just lay there on the bunk with his eyes open, struggling with all his might not to fall asleep just before reveille. Otherwise he'd flake out completely and get doused with water as well. They'd hoist him up off the bunk to go on duty and he'd have to live through three hours before he could lie back down again.

But the bastard who'd woken him was totally oblivious . . . He could have waited for his turn . . . They were lying with their sides against each other and, hearing how mightily the soldier's heart was pounding, Matiushin forced himself to think of his own heart, which he couldn't even hear beating.

When Pomogalov appeared in the sleeping area and started swearing in the darkness as he shook awake the squad that was catching up on its sleep, Matiushin realised quite distinctly that his turn had come to go out into the zone, but it took him a long time to gather the strength to tear himself off the bunk. They slept fully clothed. Matiushin pulled out his belt with the gun-clip pouch on it from under the mattress and put it on. Then he sat up on the bunk and caught his breath. He had to wind on his footcloths. But they were cold, damp with sweat. He wound them on any old how, then pulled over his terminally battered, concertinaed boots, heaved them onto his feet and was surprised at how heavy they felt, as if he'd buried his legs in the ground up to the knees.

Around him the soldiers were getting up, some in silence, some noisily, in a fury, half-blind in their drowsy state, grabbing footcloths and boots, sharing them out. Pomogalov spurred them on.

'Get out into the light, you can sort things out there!'

Matiushin was about to go, but he dawdled, suddenly remembering the soldier on the bunk he'd just left. The soldier had turned over onto his stomach, put his hands under his head, stretched out on the bunk and reached his arm across the place that Matiushin had left. The man's heart was beating regularly and his chest expanding more deeply, and that meant there was something in this life that Matiushin wouldn't get because of him. Only Matiushin didn't know what it was that he wouldn't get. And now the commander had come along and was driving Matiushin out on guard duty. But that bastard would stay there, and he'd catch up on his sleep better and faster – and Matiushin wanted to chase out the man who was sleeping. He'd missed his own turn to catch up and now he realised how strong his hatred was as he tried to make out the bitter enemy of his heart in the darkness. It looked like his enemy had caught up all right. And now Matiushin had to as well.

Matiushin started shaking the sleeping man.

'What are you doing sleeping, get out on duty!'

'But I . . . But they . . . ' The soldier tumbled over onto his side and started flailing about: a leg this way, an arm that way . . . He was trying to crawl away.

'Get up, the watch officer ordered me to get you up.'

'Fucker . . . Get off me, brother, I'm only just back from the tower . . . Go away, I'll kill you . . . '

Matiushin reluctantly took his hands off the soldier, who immediately went limp, muttering something. The only thing Matiushin could make out was that he was angry. And he was tossing about again, trying to crawl away and hide. You got what you deserve, you bastard, Matiushin thought, I gave you a good shaking. And although all his weakened insides stubbornly resisted any haste, Matiushin was so agitated that he drove himself on. As if that was what he lived for – tearing himself off a bunk and clambering back onto it.

To perk themselves up before going on duty in the zone, the soldiers drank *chifir* with the black bread left over from the evening before. Rebrov, who was lackeying in the guardhouse, prepared the *chifir*. He cut up the loaf too and sprinkled sugar on the slices. Eight men going off in the night squad, the same number as there were guard posts on the towers. Matiushin came late and was last to sit down at the table.

'Give me some chow!' he demanded.

The men sipped on their *chifir*, looking cunningly from Matiushin to the lackey and back again. Rebrov stood there shamefaced and bewildered.

'It's like this, Vasenka. The bread's all gone . . . I didn't spot that there wasn't enough.'

'What, you bastard?' Matiushin yelled in a strangled voice, sensing that everyone around him was holding their breath and waiting.

'There wasn't enough bread . . . '

Matiushin couldn't understand: how could he have been left without bread? And then suddenly he snapped . . . It was that bastard's fault, the one who woke him up early. It was his fault Matiushin didn't get any bread. And everyone around him was chewing away and supping tea. Matiushin was the only one sitting there like a fool, like a poor relative. These ugly bastards didn't seem to have hurried at all, but they'd got a good measure of every-thing – they wouldn't be feeling hungry. He suddenly fancied that the business with the bed and the bread had all been set up – they were starting to grind him down on the sly. They'd set Rebrov on him, and that freak was only too happy to oblige them.

'Well, I'll be having a word with you . . . Give me some *chifir*!'

Rebrov came to life and started pouring hastily. He was in such a hurry that he poured Matiushin's *chifir* into a light-blue mug. Everyone went quiet when he held out the blue mug to Matiushin, and Matiushin squeezed back against the bench. But Rebrov didn't understand a thing, the fool; he smiled guiltily, eager to oblige and declared:

'I brewed it up with boiling water! Really hot!'

Someone suddenly let out a laugh.

'It's Pomogalov. He's guzzling his tea and he doesn't want to drink out of the poofy blue one either!'

'How's it come to this, no decent mugs in the guardhouse!'

'Come on, suicide boy, take a sup . . . '

'I won't take what's not mine, I'll do without.'

The tower men grinned contentedly. Matiushin grinned too; it was easier for him to grin like that. They started sleepily trickling out into the guard room. Dojo and the sergeant-major were listening to the radio. The Chinese was sleepy and his head was nodding.

'What do they say on the radio, what's the weather like?'

'Hail and snow with lightning!' Pomogalov said with a weary grin and crowed with his voice breaking: 'Right then, my sons, how about a bit more marching? Anyone still alive? You screw anything up in the zone, and I can't give you a pardon. The show's over.'

'You what, you what?' Dybenko protested aggressively. 'The slightest little thing, and you start threatening. You ought to feed us properly. Just look, there wasn't even enough bread, or tea . . . '

'I know what you're like, you guzzle it all and then complain.'

Dojo asked furtively:

'Time for arm-up, comrade Commander?'

'Go ahead, arm them . . . And mind you, sergeant . . . no funny business!'

One after another the tower men plodded off to take their guns. After finding his automatic in the stand, Matiushin dragged himself out into the little guardhouse yard.

Stretched out in a line, they walked across the steppe to the camp circle. Matiushin strode out in front, so he wouldn't see anyone. They called and swore from the back, telling him not to push them so fast, but Matiushin didn't listen to them.

After pulling well ahead of the squad, he got stuck at the path to the first metal gate, which he couldn't go through without everyone else – there was an alarm on the entrance and when it was opened a siren started howling. The Chinese caught up with him at the path.

'Eh-ha . . . That not good. You get ahead us all.'

'They're creeping along like women . . . Listen, give them a good angry shout, they're a total shambles!'

'Sell quick, you must. No need sell yours, but mine needed at home. Money good. Much money needed at a home.'

'You keep going on about it, but I say – enough, leave it for a while.'

Dojo smiled and nodded his head once.

'Then give money – and all right.'

'I haven't got any.'

'E-e-e-eh . . . Not good. Sell – and will be money. Think, no money – you go to zone. Me report to commander, commander find out.'

'You Chinese bastard, you'll be shopping yourself, I won't keep my mouth shut!'

'Me no sell, Matiusa, you sell. Eh, you alone, Matiusa.'

The Chinese pulled a flask out from under his tunic and thrust it at him. Matiushin was about to push it away, but he heard the tramping of feet and grabbed it despite himself, silently hanging the weight on his belt, to one side of his clip pouch.

The men who had fallen behind started appearing out of the darkness: the trainer with an Alsatian, the two men from Khabarovsk and Dybenko, who was cheerfully driving on the sleepy, dejected local soldiers, like animals clumped together into a little herd.

'Where were you going in such a rush, guys, tearing off ahead like that?'

'Do we have to wait for you, lowlife?'

'What a night, I just can't get enough of it!'

'Ah, shut it, will you?'

'What's up, scumbags? Don't you want to rejoice in life? Is your life so full of shit?'

Matiushin swore, but he swallowed the insult. Dybenko wasn't afraid of Matiushin's oaths, but he wasn't in the mood to poke fun or start a fight either. Neither of them noticed anyone around them, screening out the others with their bodies. When the Chinese opened the entrance, Matiushin strode through decisively, first onto the path, but Dybenko hustled a cigarette from the local soldiers and dropped behind, unhurriedly puffing out smoke.

The boiler house chimney towered up above the zone and into the night, the white smoke billowing and swirling out of its soundless trumpet mouth and melting away in the cold. From the searchlights attached to the chimney like little baby spiders, two white-hot beams of light thrust out and enveloped the path, so that the soldiers moved along in a blindingly bright mist. But on the other side of the camp wall there was breathless darkness, as blank as the two-metre-high wooden boards, and immediately above the fences the night began.

By the time they'd covered a good part of the path and come to the sequence of guard towers, the nerves of the men in the squad were jangling. They had all sobered up from their sleep, feeling the feather-lightness of their bodies, loaded down only by the weight of their automatics and the shuddering cold. One man fell back, one lengthened his stride, one held his pace in silent fury; the line of walking men levelled out and closed up, and the man whose turn it was to climb up the tower to his post was shoved forward to close in on it face to face.

When they stopped at the first tower, started talking and livened up a bit, a soldier stuck his head out of the tower and roared deafeningly.

'I've frozen solid waiting to be relieved! Did you dig in at the guardhouse, you scumbags?'

Another soldier was already clambering up into the tower and forcing himself to look back behind him, at the path, but no one called to him. The one who'd been yelling, a big strapping guy, came slithering down, flopped onto Dybenko's chest, half-stunned, and wheezed right into his mouth:

'Vasyok, give us a smoke! I'm gasping, brothers, a drag at least!'

The trainer led the Alsatian on along the path. The fourth tower was at a spot like a dead-end, blank and dark, where the fences closed together at an angle, choking off the path like a vice. The trainer skulked along, signalling for them to stop with a wave of his hand. No one could make out what he was afraid of, but they all went quiet and completed the path in agonised suspense.

At the tower they got their breath back and relaxed when they realised what was going on.

'He's asleep,' the trainer reported in a whisper and fell silent, waiting for what would come next.

The tower was shrouded in the bright haze of the guard-post lamps. They were sideways on, so that the soldier's black figure could be seen in the opening of the tower's square box. The soldier was sleeping on his feet, with his head lowered.

'Who is it?' the Chinese asked in a low voice.

'Some beast . . . ' Dybenko whispered behind his back.

'Young, sleeping so soundly and sweetly. Ah, he needs a fix. Maybe I'll go up and take him while he's wasted . . . '

The trainer stayed with the Alsatian – he squatted down and put his arm round the dog, choking it slightly so that it wouldn't make any sudden movements.

Dybenko and the Chinese crept towards the tower. During those long moments the cold caught up with Matiushin and the other waiting soldiers and they started feeling chilly. For some reason the sergeant stopped at the steps and Dybenko climbed up the tower alone, disappearing into the half-light. As Matiushin watched Dybenko climbing the steps like a hunter, drawing out the sweetness of it, he started trembling as the passion awoke in him to yell out at the top of his voice. Why, never mind; yell! He'd slip the automatic off his shoulder, strip this lot naked and make them dance!

The sleeping soldier didn't sense anything. He was lost in his dreams. Matiushin didn't feel sorry for him, he just didn't want to get stuck here waiting. This dopehead meant nothing but delay for Matiushin. Suddenly he heard the dopehead shriek and actually saw the tower shudder bodily. The Chinese shouted something, everybody relaxed and moved closer along the path, exchanging mocking comments. Laughing, Dybenko kicked the hophead head first down the steep steps from the tower. When he slithered off them the Chinese set about him, not giving him a chance to stand up. The soldier came to life and shuddered with joy at falling into the hands of his own kind. Realising they were making fun of him, he played up to them, babbling away in his own language. The trainer moved aside, restraining the growling Alsatian, and grinned. He'd been going to set about the dopehead seriously but he could see they'd turned it into a bit of fun. The dopehead rolled about, grunting, enough to make you die laughing; he writhed about as if he was dying and they didn't have the heart to trample on him.

Matiushin just stood there, waiting. But they were enjoying themselves; they were in no hurry to abandon their fun. And then he couldn't take any more. He pushed the frozen brutes aside, stepping through from behind their backs, gazing with a painful ferocity at the dopehead writhing at his feet, and struck him a dull blow with the butt of his rifle, as if to crush him. The dopehead gave a shrill squeal, clutched his head and lay still, whining.

Dybenko started back.

'What did you slug him for, we were having fun . . . ' he said, and started helping the dopehead up off the ground.

The soldier struggled with all his strength to stay on his feet. The blood oozing out of his head was thicker than his short-cropped hair so it didn't run off but froze above his forehead in a brownish patch the size of a five-kopeck coin; he still had his smile, although now it looked guilty. He didn't believe they wouldn't carry on beating him. Dojo had kept out of things until this moment, but he came dashing in to restore order and they walked on in silence, moving round the camp, with the fences and the wire closing them into a circle without an exit, which they could only walk on round, from tower to tower. The squad crept on like a single caterpillar track and Matiushin a part of it.

Now he fancied that he was crawling, not marching. He was disgusted by the painful realisation that he hadn't achieved anything by taking out the dopehead, but was still dragging himself along even more agonisingly with all the others: as painfully as if he was the one who had been stunned by the rifle butt. Panting and not marching but jerking himself forward, he gradually fell behind, failing as his strength ran out. He needed to get up that vodka tower and get through his watch as quickly as possible – and then they'd let him sleep, sleep, sleep . . . This muttering was enough to relax Matiushin a little bit, but it was just like when he was drifting in his sleep, he felt as if he was being crushed, squeezed up, shoved aside, and he filled with a trembling that was like little lead pellets. It was that other one who was sleeping, it was him, the bastard. That was what it was: *he* was sleeping. The trembling ran through Matiushin, its little pellets bit into his body and, in the grip of this deadly inner chill, Matiushin grew frightened, as if he was starting to drown and die.

*

As soon as they reached the vodka tower, despondency swept over the other soldiers as well; the Chinese and the men from the other squad drove Matiushin on so they wouldn't have to dawdle. They wanted to get away from this lousy place as soon as possible. Matiushin shared the watch on the vodka tower with a tame young soldier whose name no one in the company even knew. Matiushin was the only one who associated with him, as his watch partner. The soldier was clutching his automatic in his arms and mumbling something mournfully, endlessly. Matiushin climbed up the tower. He'd have to explain to the creature that his time was up – otherwise he wouldn't even realise it and would spend the whole night there. Matiushin had to hit him so it hurt, then he'd understand and the fear would make him clear out. But when this creature had to take over from Matiushin it was just the opposite; he would stare down stubbornly at the ground and not move a step until the sergeant overseeing the changeover drove him up the tower with his fists.

Someone shouted up after Matiushin:

'Don't sleep, Matiukha, or you'll get fucked!'

The soldiers didn't wait for them. The squad moved on, flowing away hurriedly along the path into the darkness in which the guardhouse was already glimmering.

'Fuck off out of it!' Matiushin yelled, kicking out with his boot.

The soldier huddled into a corner and started keening something pitifully.

'Come on, or I'll give you some real hassle!' cried Matiushin, ready to throw himself at him.

The little soldier calmed down. And he was moved to say something: to complain. Matiushin calmed down himself and agreed.

'You're right there ... Hang in there, hang in there ... The two of us know it: you and me are going to die here ... '

The beast's eyes were glazed and dim, but suddenly they flashed, and he shed a tear as he realised something, or perhaps took fright again. Then he couldn't hold back and started bawling in his fear. And Matiushin hit him hard right in the very soul, in the pit of the stomach.

'I'll kill you, you bastard, get out of here!'

When the soldier disappeared from view, it grew dark on the vodka tower. It had been black before, but now it turned even blacker. Matiushin looked round desolately at the realm he was meant to guard. The railway branch line from the zone ran right next to the tower and the round form of the convicts' hospital loomed up out of the blackness. Only a vague outline of everything was visible now: walls that weren't walls, rails that weren't rails, ground that wasn't quite ground ... And this was the point where the great expanse of the steppe, which from morning to night stretched out wider than the sky, withdrew from the camp territory to wait at the guard-post lamps: even the strength of its vastness wasn't enough against their no-man's-land, hard-labour light.

At night the warders would be led out of the zone. A handful would be left as a formal presence and they'd shut themselves in as securely as possible and wait for the morning. Because the branch line ran by there, the exclusion zone and the barriers were absolutely negligible at the vodka tower. Here a convict could spit in the soldier's face and leap over all the barriers in a single bound. Never mind flasks – you could drive a tractor along the rails into the zone without leaving even a trace, and no one would hear.

Matiushin felt like running away from the vodka tower, but he kept standing there. Only the tower room didn't suit his height. In order to stay standing, he either had to slump over lopsidedly against the wall or bend his head down. He twisted himself round and lit a cigarette, feeling inconsolably angry. Life was shit because it was a long march to the vodka tower and, when you got there, there wasn't enough space to live in. And nothing to look at, and nothing to think about.

While you were content with just one square foot of land in the world, you stood on just that one square foot. But the moment you looked up at the sky, you scraped your dirty face against its vastness. And you felt so vile: the most you could ever do on your own little patch of land was choke on it or defile it. You were a low, creeping creature in these expanses, and you'd been given a square foot of ground as an act of mercy. But how can you live if you hate life itself? You'll live with a struggle, in a fury . . . Croak? No damn way! Shove over? *You* go and croak!

But the wind lashes at your face and hurtles off into the steppe, and breathing against its blast is frightening – you start gasping and it rips open your chest from the inside. There's the wind driving along a huge cloud of dust, there it is straining against a guard tower, setting it cracking and humming. And it comes hurtling out of everywhere, and thrashes about everywhere, as if it's seeking refuge, but the space is so vast that it goes rushing on impetuously.

He heard a rustling sound close by and a convict who looked like he was bricked into his clothes limped out into the light of the guard-post lamp, making no attempt to hide. Looking closely at him, Matiushin slipped the automatic off his shoulder just in case, but he decided that there was nothing to be alarmed about: maybe it was some deadbeat from the hospital – they sometimes came out and staggered about at night, for the fresh air. Then the convict relaxed, squatted down and stretched out his gnarled hands, as if warming himself at a little campfire.

'Well, lad, how's army life?'

'What do you want?' Matiushin snarled.

'I'm waiting for the shop to open. I need a drink. Sell me something . . . ' the convict whined. 'I'll pay top price, lad, sell me something – I'll die otherwise . . . '

'All right. Twenty roubles, and you'll have your booze. Throw it in under the tower. They'll pick it up there. But you'll have to wait,' Matiushin hissed. He saw a little bundle fly through the air.

The convict silently turned away from Matiushin and walked back into the darkness of the zone.

Matiushin suddenly choked. It was a gust of wind, setting the camp beating its knotted living shadow, its ragged, dishevelled head, against the ground until it swelled up with black blood, and then reeling back into the night, as if it drew strength and solidity from this blood. Sensing intuitively that this was a turbulence of the air, that somewhere in the steppe the winds had clashed, hurtling together precipitately from all sides of the world, and their currents and their lightning bolts, hewn out of the steppe, would pound at the camp – at the chimneys, the beacons and the guard towers – Matiushin sat down on the floor of his little hut, where it was like being in a coffin. He lit a cigarette with chilly fingers, no longer hearing the wind's howls but a profound silence. Drying himself out with the warmth of the smoke, dragging it in deeper and harder, in order not to fall asleep, Matiushin didn't doze or sink into a tobacco stupor but dreamed timelessly and motionlessly. Suddenly what had been tormenting him unawares ever since he woke rose up clearly and simply out of his weakened entrails: last night he had grown tired of the time he had lived and the time he still had to live – deadly tired. And even if that desperate young guy hadn't shoved him off the bunk, he would still have gone off onto the path, dragging this deadly weight with him, thinking in his shuddering impatience that he could overcome it, finally defeat it. And instead of selling moonshine, scurrying about with it night after night, he felt like getting drunk on it and burying himself in the steppe, in order to sleep soundly through at least one night.

Yet at this point something stronger than his own will, some other fear, like a second wind, made him tense up and jump to his feet. The zone stood there docilely in its twilight rows of barriers. Not a sound, not a rustle on all sides apart from the noise of the wind. However, this order and silence in the night was a quiet torment to Matiushin, destroying his peace. He looked out and listened, uncertain what he was preparing for but remembering that the vodka tower was due for a visit.

A minute later, from the next tower after his, the one that completed the circle round the camp and stood right beside the guardhouse, there was the hoot of a challenge – the guard there had passed the test, he hadn't slept through it. But they were moving round the path in reverse, not the regulation way, because the reverse route to him was less visible and shorter – and the shout warned him that the vodka tower would soon have visitors too. He waited for a man to appear out of the distant darkness of someone else's guard post, but soon heard the jerky, gurgling breathing of an Alsatian that seemed to surface from under the ground and fixed its eyes on the steep spire of the watch tower, throwing its head back as if howling silently. The Alsatian was guarding Matiushin for the trainer, who had let it off the lead, sending it on far ahead to reconnoitre at the vodka tower; if any warders came close on the zone side to check, if there was even one living soul anywhere nearby, the Alsatian would do its job and start barking; the trainer would know that the coast wasn't clear and he ought to march past the tower without stopping.

Matiushin made out the trainer and the titchy Chinese hurrying after him, afraid to march in front for some reason. The closer they came, the harder Matiushin found it to breathe. And when the sergeant and the trainer drew completely level with the tower, so that Matiushin could hear the Chinese panting and his automatic and accessories jangling, all he felt was the oppression of a boredom and a depression that were infinitely alike. He was bored because he knew everything and depressed because the Chinese simply wouldn't calm down, he kept on twitching and jangling mournfully, as if he was stuffed full of copper coins.

Dojo broke the silence by calling Matiushin quietly from the path, but only to make sure that there was no need for him to climb up the tower. Matiushin responded. Dojo asked, perhaps mockingly, if the flask had been sold and received the unexpected reply that it had. The trainer stood there, still and contemptuous, but he had to look sharp and restrain the Alsatian when the Chinese clambered in under the tower to look for the bundle that had been tossed there. Matiushin heard him panting and rummaging about and started feeling nervous himself: when would the Chinese find the little bundle?

Then it seemed to him that they were already dividing up the money, right there on the path: the Chinese handed the bundle to the trainer – the Chinese couldn't even count properly – and they whispered together about who should get how much, and maybe how to settle past debts too. Matiushin understood that, he'd been through it all himself and so, although the sergeant and the trainer had forgotten about him, he squinted at the zone and kept his guard up – thinking that he was involved in this deal. But suddenly the tower shuddered – the trainer was climbing up for a talk.

The steps sounded closer and closer, heavier and more sombre.

'There's no money. There was only a stone in it,' Matiushin suddenly heard the trainer say in a repulsive whisper outside the little door.

Matiushin didn't believe it, knowing the trainer's habit of joking to jangle the nerves of men he was afraid of touching for real – as if he wanted to grind them down by instilling uncertainty and fear. But the trainer wasn't joking, he asked rapidly and angrily who had ordered the moonshine and then, not believing a word Matiushin said, he hissed:

'Decided to rat on us, have you? Did you think Dojo and me wouldn't stick our noses into your burrow? Do you know what you get for that? You lose everything. Got that, you rat . . . You've pissed everyone off, no one's going to put up with anything from you any longer.'

It went quiet. Soon the guard on the next tower called out – the trainer and the Chinese had walked on to that one, as if crossing over to another shore. At that deep, dark hour the smooth, quiet surface of the night seemed to be hemmed in between two shores, two widely severed patches of the dry steppe. Matiushin felt as if everything was drifting away into the night, becoming strange and hopelessly distant. And the vodka tower had stepped down into this smooth surface of the night and was moving away and away, completely strange and alien to everyone.

Matiushin shuddered as if he'd been scalded – so they'd already decided his fate . . . And he only had until tomorrow left. He saw very clearly what would happen and how it would happen if he was relieved from the tower, went back to the guardhouse and never came back to the tower again. He saw it in the few minutes that it took him to live through the whole of the next day that had already started, during which he would be betrayed to Arman, and Arman would arrest him and send him under armed guard to Karaganda, to a cell in the pre-trial detention centre. After going without sleep for the fourth night in a row, more dead than alive, Matiushin suddenly felt himself retreating rapidly from life with the ease of despair, into a kind of non-existence; as if he was beginning to sleep with his eyes open, seeing dreams, but not living.

In the space of a minute Matiushin also saw the thieves in the prison torturing him, a soldier, in a cell as tight and narrow as a womb. And the firm determination to shoot himself was exposed, like the bottom of his soul, drawn into the funnel of a crater. He had to shoot himself, he understood that quite definitely, in order not to die in prison or in the zone, and because he knew everything in advance; that there was only the crushing monolith of the last day that had already begun, hatched out of the soft top of this night's head, with the vodka tower standing there on top of its mountain, still standing there. At that moment Matiushin's automatic became everything to him. Its weight had long since sunk into his shoulder, into his body, and it no longer weighed anything without Matiushin, it was cotton wool, it merely warmed his side. Death from its bullet enticed Matiushin with this kind warmth, arousing no resistance or even fear. The only frightening thing would be to leave it too late and suddenly find himself in the guardhouse, where they would disarm him and place him under arrest. Once his soul had reached this extreme boundary, as if he had passed the final circle of his own terrible non-existence, Matiushin recovered consciousness and immediately jerked the breech block.

The entire impenetrable abyss of the zone froze with not one of the thousand eyes of its lights blinking, with every one stabbing its bright ray into him.

He remembered about the flask: it had appeared in order to be drunk at this moment, as if this were its appointed destiny.

He thought that he would smoke and swig from the flask, and then shoot himself. He measured that fate out for himself, and then he lit up . . . The flask, still plump with weight, brought him to his senses for a moment, inspiring the sudden thought that he mustn't drink. He absolutely mustn't, although he couldn't understand what point there was in forbidding himself to drink. But he shuddered and gulped down the liquid from the flask, choking on it, until he had drained it completely, still-ing the fear of imminent death and feeling as if he had warmed himself up. His farewell thought was that he had got drunk – and no one would punish him for it. Holding this thought inside him like a gulp of air, Matiushin sank down onto the bottom of his box, jolly at the thought of his own fearlessness, and started smoking his final ciga-rette. He believed that he was acting against some kind of untruth, that he was still fighting – and he would win. They wanted something else from him, for him to submit, to resign himself to things and to live entangled on all sides in fears and debts. They had sheltered behind his fear but now they would have to scurry and suffer, the way he had suffered while they were guzzling and sleep-ing. He was going to shoot himself – and the vodka tower would collapse. They were the ones who'd go on trial, they were the ones who'd be put under guard tomorrow, and Arman would be punished too, he wouldn't be an officer any more, they'd find out the truth about him. And they'd drive someone else up the vodka tower instead of Matiushin – one of those who were willing to betray him. And the ones who weren't driven up it would see this trial, and the fear of what they'd seen would be more agonising than the trial itself, and longer.

He didn't feel it when the cigarette of death burned out in his fingers . . . The night went by. He saw the shimmering airy expanse open up and the chimney pierce the white clouds in the milky, twilight currents of the sky. A chilly, leaden wakefulness flooded through his veins and he grabbed tight hold of his automatic, but suddenly something struck the tower – someone had tossed a stone – and Matiushin jumped to his feet, plunging forward without a thought, bouncing up like a spring, afraid of not getting it done in time, before they bellowed out the reveille.

In the morning silence, which was as desolate as the air, Matiushin sensed someone hiding there, breathing, close to the vodka tower, someone with whom he was intimately bound by the silence.

Matiushin discerned his presence with an intuition that wasn't human, as if the convict was a pinched nerve in Matiushin's body. The convict didn't come closer to the tower but waited: not simply looking but peeking out from somewhere at one side, like a bare, stunted little tree in this morning half-light. And he was swaying like a little tree. Their eyes met when the convict staggered and stepped forward awkwardly, as if he'd missed his footing.

That moment's burden of silence and emptiness was more than Matiushin could bear. He even fancied that there was no convict, only a grey pillar. But the pillar suddenly came to life and backed away – and the morning surfaced again, buoyant and airy in its colourlessness.

Sensing something, the convict started walking away, trying to put some distance between himself and the tower. Matiushin was standing like a soldier now – like a two-legged gun made of something solid, heavy and immobile. As he watched, it was getting lighter with every minute. It was as if he was inside a bright, empty, deserted barracks hut. Only it had an earth floor and was roofed in solidly by the sky. He could hear its wooden boards groaning and the draughts droning in its chimney, and the air smelled of the boards' uninhabited forests, the dampness of the sky, the earth, and there was an old smell of a man from the corners, like the dust of bones. Suddenly the searchlights and lamps went out around the zone's entire perimeter. The master switch had been thrown in the guardhouse and the morning turned dark and cold, as if it had been overgrown by thunder clouds. A cold order was instilled in everything, as if the rows of barracks, fences and towers had been connected to an electric current. The camp morning had arrived. But the convict suddenly surfaced again out of the calm, bright, smooth emptiness.

Matiushin called to him, afraid of frightening him off . . .

The convict waited a while and started moving towards the vodka tower, staggering and zigzagging. It was hard for him to manage his lame leg, which either trailed behind him or jammed against something, like a stick. Maybe it was this difficulty that made him stand there crookbacked, looking furtively back over the steps he had taken, then straighten up and move on towards the vodka tower. And while the convict was dragging himself along, Matiushin threw the empty flask down under the tower – for him. It clattered lightly, but the convict didn't make a dash for it, he stopped fearfully when he heard that sound.

'Well, what have you stopped for? It's yours, all paid for . . . Come on, quick now. It's no distance at all from you, further over to the right, over to the right!'

'Na-ah . . . I can't see it . . . Na-ah . . . ' the convict complained agonisingly, but then, with the same agony in every step, he crept out from behind the gate, straight along the sleepers onto the bare, stony space right under the tower, and suddenly flung himself on the flask after all. At that moment, when the convict emerged into the bright emptiness of the spot that had been created in order to swat a man like a fly, not giving him any chance to come to his senses, take cover or dodge away from death, Matiushin felt a repulsively sickening ease. Without even taking aim, he sensed the convict's animal warmth and blindly swung the automatic in the direction of this little man, this cornered, fragile, gristly little animal – and he felt as if he was going insane, he couldn't decide what to do, didn't know who to punish and what for. But then the convict grabbed the flask and stood rooted to the spot for a moment with his head thrown back, so that Matiushin could see his eyes glinting like two bright coins, frozen in terror. Looking into those eyes, Matiushin froze too, stunned. The convict turned back. His lame, infirm leg twisted under him, he collapsed and attempted to crawl away – but the shots were already roaring out . . . The convict was spun round by the detonations, no longer alive, but dodging away from the bullets, unwilling to die. But when the breech jerked emptily and jammed, the bullet-riddled body went limp and settled into eternal peace at that one empty click.

Matiushin released the automatic from his hands as if setting an animal free. Totally blank, he tumbled down inside the wooden box, breathing in the lead-grey gunpowder smoke that had settled onto its floor. Deafened, he couldn't hear anything, but the tramping of boots came closer and closer. The guards were dashing to the vodka tower. Their calling voices reached him on the wind. The barking of the Alsatians merged with the human voices, only it seemed to be cascading down from the sky, from somewhere up on high. But Matiushin, in his blank isolation, started crying like a little child. The tears flowed and he gaped blindly, not knowing why he was crying. But it felt calm and warm.

*

The zone shuddered at the shots on the vodka tower.

The convicts, the entire thousand of them, went wild. They could hear the Alsatians barking. They could hear the boots tramping.

The alarm had brought out the guard!

Matiushin was dragged down off the tower, totally dazed. The convict was lying in the exclusion zone and Pomogalov was prowling round the body on his own. He picked up the flask and hid it – then moved away from the body, advancing on Matiushin, slapped him round the face and yelled:

'Are you a man or a hysterical woman? Big deal, so you've blown away an escaper. I've blown away a dozen of them – and I'm fine.' He called the Chinese in a hoarse voice and ordered the sergeant to hide Matiushin away out of sight in the guardhouse. 'That's right, that's right – drag him onto a bunk, let him catch up on his sleep, out of sight.' They lugged Matiushin through the cordon by his arms. The soldiers hanging about in the wind examined him and grinned. They'd already heard and were amazed that the suicide boy had shot a convict; only yesterday evening no one even imagined that destiny could hand him anything like that.

They led him to the guardhouse and the silence there was deathly: the soldiers didn't know what to say to Matiushin. They seemed afraid, as if it wasn't Matiushin at all but a werewolf. They couldn't even talk to each other. And at the slightest hint that Matiushin would have to be given leave for his runaway, every man felt a huge stony lump rising up in his throat – who ever finds it sweet to talk about his own shattered dream? They just slapped Matiushin on the shoulder or ruffled his hair: good lad, you didn't foul it up. But Matiushin didn't believe it. He fancied they were being sly, trying to put him off his guard, that they were toying with him but they knew the truth. They knew, they knew, they knew . . . Just one more moment and he'd go down at his comrades' feet. Brothers, mates, stop torturing me! I wouldn't have dared, I didn't want to, it was him, the bastard, he tricked me! But Pomogalov came dashing into the guardhouse, black in the face with all his cares. He saw that Matiushin wasn't sleeping, but wandering about, working himself up to puke, and almost drove him out with his fists.

'You're going to be interrogated!' he shouted. 'Do you hear? I want you ready for interrogation, get out of here, go and sleep!'

'I didn't want to . . . ' Matiushin started whinging, almost giving himself away. 'It was him . . . '

But Pomogalov yelled:

'You're a hero, you fucker, understand? You have to be a hero for me, for the whole company. Go and get washed! Sleep! It's all over, your war's finished! As soon as we've logged the body, you're going home to rest. You've got nothing to be afraid of. No one's going to touch you. That's it, lad, consider that you've served your time. And if you start whining – I'll smash your face.'

He crept into the wash room, thinking he'd escaped from pursuit. But there was Rebrov scouring dishes with the abrasive local water. When he saw Matiushin he shuddered, thinking Matiushin was going to beat him for what had happened with the bread ration.

'Vasenka . . . ' he babbled, 'it was the trainer, he told me to give him your ration, and I didn't mean to do that with the mug, it won't happen again.'

Matiushin didn't hear what Vanka was saying. What ration, what trainer – no, that wasn't the way it was! Afraid of frightening off the groveller, Matiushin put his arms round him and pulled him close so that he wouldn't run away.

'Ah, you're all bastards . . . Reckon everything's turned out your way, do you?'

'What's turned out what way, Vasya? It was the trainer, the trainer told me to.'

'The trainer? Told you? What did he tell you?'

'Nothing, nothing . . . '

'You're lying. You know. Everyone knows. But I won't give in that easily. I'll do for the lot of you here. I've got nothing to lose.'

Without even realising it, he really was strangling Rebrov, squeezing tighter and tighter. As he wheezed, Rebrov suddenly understood that he was being strangled to death and jerked desperately, throwing Matiushin over, so that he was able to tear himself free and go running off. Matiushin darted after him, but he collided with a wall.

He came to in a corner of the dark, blank watch corridor that was like a crack between two walls, and didn't know which way to run.

As he fumbled about in the dark, his hand disappeared through a black, open doorway, and he immediately caught the smell of foot cloths stabbing out of it, and heard the resounding silence of human breathing.

This was the doorway Matiushin had kept dashing to round the circle of the camp. And last night he hadn't got enough sleep. Every time he collapsed lifeless onto the bunk, thinking that this was the night when he would catch up on his sleep and break free from his leaden, pitch-black drowsiness, as if he'd only ever agreed to live because he'd been promised that half his life would be sleep.

Matiushin had been dashing along the path to the vodka tower. He wanted to get there quickly. But now there was a roaring in his head and he was trapped in this crack, in this opening that breathed out drowsiness. And now there was nowhere to dash to, and no one would ever bother him again, they wouldn't call his name to get him up for duty – they'd go without him.

The darkness and isolation in the sleeping area was the kind that can probably only exist underground. He started moving forward, forcing himself against the wall. He pressed up against a bunk-bed that he could smell and hear, and tumbled onto it, fancying that he was tumbling into a top bunk where a dozen soldiers, invisible in the dark, but just like him, were welded together in a drowsy crush.

His living and suffering were over.

'That's all now . . . It's the end . . . ' Matiushin just had time to think before someone prodded him in the stomach and shook him, straining to heave him off the bunk.

'Shove over! I'll kill you, you bastard!'

Matiushin tried to say his own name. He mumbled. He resisted. He felt as if his soul was being shaken out of him. They were torturing him. They'd started the interrogation.

And he summoned up all his willpower and groaned: 'Kill me, kill me . . . '

And he heard:

'Get up! Come on! Shift off the bunk, you pushy bastard! It's not your time yet!'

They shoved him out into the light, under a lamp, and he found himself in the watch officer's room, unable to tell if it was day or night, and how long they'd let him sleep. Pomogalov was standing there, skulking in the swampy darkness of his crumpled tunic. Arman was sitting at the desk, looking as if he'd been chopped off at the waist . . . He was leading the interrogation. Then he jumped to his feet. In his impatience he moved right up close, shouting something, flexing his arm and finally swinging it back – but Pomogalov suddenly shielded Matiushin from the officer with his own body.

'Why put the young lad through this? You've seen the body, you know what happened. Have you really no idea what you're after, what you're getting yourself into? Show him some pity; how's he going to live now? And if you don't want to, comrade Senior Lieutenant, pardon me, but it's time to put an end to this! This is the lad's fourth day on guard duty . . . You make me sick. You've got other things to think about! The zone's mutinied! You'll have blood, and there'll be plenty of it!'

Arman froze – and then called loudly for the soldiers. The sergeant-major laughed and Matiushin, clutching at this jolly laugh of disbelief, shook his head, staring off somewhere into empty space. No one came in response to the political officer's call. Arman waited in the silence for about a minute and then gave another order, this time to Pomogalov.

'Come with me.'

Matiushin was left alone. He waited so long that everything inside him collapsed, and some time later the sergeant-major came into the little room on his own, seeming very strange, looking at Matiushin with a mournful and helpless expression.

'Son, something's happened. Be strong now son, be strong . . . ' But tears that seemed grey, as if they had grey skins, were seeping out of his eyes. 'We got a telegram by phone; your old man, your father, has died . . . *He* had the telegram yesterday already . . . So that's it, these things happen. You be strong now, but just have a little

cry here, come on now . . . Only don't you do anything to
yourself, you understand, do you hear me? I swear on my
daughter that you'll leave this place today. It says you're
to be demobilised; he's got no more right. Well, do you
want me to go and shoot him? Do you want me to shoot
myself, bastard that I am? Have you gone deaf, or what?
Don't just say nothing!'

EPILOGUE

Final reminiscences

At the bus station a motley crowd of people was jostling and yelling beside a colourless concrete-and-glass box, and a large, white, human-looking dog was suffering torment in the biting cold, tethered by a rope to a birch tree that looked fragile in its coating of hoarfrost. The dog's owner had forgotten about it – he was probably jostling in that crowd. But the thought occurred to Matiushin that this was a simple, clear way to get rid of an animal that was no longer wanted; not throw it out, because then it would hang about outside the building and never leave you in peace, but walk a good distance away and tie it up in a well-populated spot, even beside a shop. Then either someone would take a fancy to it and steal it, or it would freeze, standing in the same spot overnight, and croak, and that same night it would be covered over by a snowdrift, so it wouldn't bother your conscience. And all day long it would strain on its rope, it wouldn't even whine, but bark in wild desperation that it was being killed, only none of the passers-by would understand that it had been left there to die, not just for a minute, and that this barking was its death howl. He'd just got off the bus that had brought him here and was glancing around, waiting for his eyes to stumble across the slip road leading off the highway, the road that his mother had explained to him about . . . And before that they'd walked to the 'Soviet' cemetery to tell them that they were burying someone and arranged things there. Matiushin had felt good there, in that quiet nook, although his mother had made him dress up for the first time in the sheepskin coat and the deerskin cap and boots that had turned out to be just his size, the ones his father had kept for five years and hardly even worn, buying everything for himself in larger sizes out of thrift. Matiushin had walked round the cemetery, constrained by the unfamiliar sheepskin coat and still unaccustomed to civilian clothes, far away from his brother's snow-covered grave, and delighted in the glittering, untouched snow, feeling in his father's clothes as if he was wearing the living family armour. There was no sense of dread, as if this wasn't a cemetery but a winter garden. The snowdrifts on the graves brought peace to the earth and the dead in that earth. At his brother's grave, where his mother talked respectfully to a watchman the same age as herself, he stood a little distance away, listening to their complaints about their health, and suddenly thought: if he'd been killed or died before his brother, he'd have been lying here. But now his father would be buried with his brother – and they'd be together here for all eternity.

He walked round the crowd and the glass box, waddling heavily as he made his way out onto the empty white road ploughed up slightly by cars and buses, where he could already make out the tall chimney of the crematorium with its fragile plume of grey smoke. As he strode along, he was thinking obstinately about just one thing now – that he would untie the dog on his way back and let it find its own way home or find its master. The office smelled of pine needles and was tended by a young girl who looked out boldly through the small window with her little baby-face. When Matiushin saw the small, toy-like, brown plastic urn he fell silent in sudden, childish surprise. The unwieldy bag that he had brought, crusted with ice, seemed both ugly and too large, and he felt so awkward that he broke into a sweat, but he didn't have any other bag. And he strode back along the road to the bus station, hearing the urn rattling about and feeling as if he himself were crusting over with ice at every step. But the dog had disappeared. There were the fresh holes of tracks in the snow by the birch tree, and the pit that the dog had dug and packed down as a lair for itself was empty. Feeling as if his suffering was over, he walked past that same crowd, that glass-and-concrete box, that same line of living, reddish-brown buses, wreathed in clouds of steam, and felt something greater than peace. He fancied that he had left this life exactly as he arrived in this world when he was born: without feeling anything.

Dear readers,

We rely on subscriptions from people like you to tell these other stories – the types of stories most publishers consider too risky to take on.

Our subscribers don't just make the books physically happen. They also help us approach booksellers, because we can demonstrate that our books already have readers and fans. And they give us the security to publish in line with our values, which are collaborative, imaginative and 'shamelessly literary'.

All of our subscribers:

- receive a first-edition copy of each of the books they subscribe to
- are thanked by name at the end of these books
- are warmly invited to contribute to our plans and choice of future books

BECOME A SUBSCRIBER, OR GIVE A SUBSCRIPTION TO A FRIEND

Visit andotherstories.org/subscribe to become part of an alternative approach to publishing.

Subscriptions are:

£20 for two books per year

£35 for four books per year

£50 for six books per year

OTHER WAYS TO GET INVOLVED

If you'd like to know about upcoming events and reading groups (our foreign-language reading groups help us choose books to publish, for example) you can:

- join the mailing list at: andotherstories.org/join-us
- follow us on Twitter: @andothertweets
- join us on Facebook: facebook.com/AndOtherStoriesBooks
- follow our blog: Ampersand

Current & Upcoming Books

01 DOWN THE RABBIT HOLE
Juan Pablo Villalobos / translated from the Spanish by Rosalind Harvey

02 ALL THE LIGHTS
Clemens Meyer / translated from the German by Katy Derbyshire

03 SWIMMING HOME
Deborah Levy

04 OPEN DOOR
Iosi Havilio / translated from the Spanish by Beth Fowler

05 HAPPINESS IS POSSIBLE
Oleg Zaionchkovsky / translated from the Russian by Andrew Bromfield

06 THE ISLANDS
Carlos Gamerro / translated from the Spanish by Ian Barnett

07 ZBINDEN'S PROGRESS
Christoph Simon / translated from the German by Donal McLaughlin

08 LIGHTNING RODS
Helen DeWitt

09 BLACK VODKA: TEN STORIES
Deborah Levy

10 CAPTAIN OF THE STEPPE
Oleg Pavlov / translated from the Russian by Ian Appleby

11 ALL DOGS ARE BLUE
Rodrigo de Souza Leão
translated from the Portuguese by Zoë Perry & Stefan Tobler

12 QUESADILLAS
Juan Pablo Villalobos / translated from the Spanish by Rosalind Harvey

13 PARADISES
Iosi Havilio / translated from the Spanish by Beth Fowler

14 DOUBLE NEGATIVE
Ivan Vladislavić

15 A MAP OF TULSA
Benjamin Lytal

16 THE RESTLESS SUPERMARKET
Ivan Vladislavić

17 SWORN VIRGIN
Elvira Dones / translated from the Italian by Clarissa Botsford

18 THE MATIUSHIN CASE
Oleg Pavlov / translated from the Russian by Andrew Bromfield

19 NOWHERE PEOPLE
Paulo Scott / translated from the Portuguese by Daniel Hahn

20 AN AMOROUS DISCOURSE IN THE SUBURBS OF HELL
Deborah Levy

21 BY NIGHT THE MOUNTAIN BURNS
Juan Tomás Ávila Laurel / translated from the Spanish by Jethro Soutar

22 THE ALPHABET OF BIRDS
SJ Naudé / translated from the Afrikaans by the author

23 ESPERANZA STREET
Niyati Keni

24 SIGNS PRECEDING THE END OF THE WORLD
Yuri Herrera / translated from the Spanish by Lisa Dillman

25 THE ADVENTURE OF THE BUSTS OF EVA PERÓN
Carlos Gamerro / translated from the Spanish by Ian Barnett

Title: *The Matiushin Case*
Author: Oleg Pavlov
Translator: Andrew Bromfield
Editor: Sophie Lewis
Typesetting & Proofreading: Tetragon, London
Series & Cover Design: Joseph Harries